Tetrasomy Two

Tetrasomy Two

BY OSCAR ROSSITER

DOUBLEDAY & COMPANY, INC.

GARDEN CITY, NEW YORK

1974

All of the characters in this book are fictitious, and any resemblance to actual persons, living or dead, is purely coincidental.

ISBN: 0-385-07732-7
Library of Congress Catalog Card Number 73–83666
Copyright © 1974 by Doubleday & Company, Inc.
FIRST EDITION

To Lois

1

IF DR. HAHN is right and "Lack of insight in psychosis signifies a poor prognosis," this is a waste of time, for you, not for me. I'm not wasting my time while I keep those electrodes away. I've had it up to here with EST (electric shock therapy), or up to here, or right through here.

I'm not going to convince you I'm well even though you used to come to me for advice now and then. You're not about to ask, "Say, Steve, I've got this first-year resident with delusions you wouldn't believe." No, you couldn't say that. "I've got this first-year resident who's had a bad trip. What do I do with him?" I'd say, "Let him leave, and leave yourself while you're about it. It's unhealthy being indoors all the time cooped up with kooks." But it isn't as easy as that; we have to go through the formalities.

The first thing we do when we start psychotherapy is state our goals. Right? Only you should have said that, not me. You're the one who's been here three years and is almost ready for private practice. Well, ready or not, here you come, huh.

Don't take umbrage, take two. I apologize. I'll settle down.

1

My goal is not to convince you I'm well, only harmless—or more so on the outside than I am in here. So when you give me demerits for bizarre ideas like being able to turn my mind up and down like a radio, don't forget to give me credit for telling you about them.

And while we are talking about things for you to label delusional material, you can add this: I know what you're going to do before you do it. Did you ever play the game when you were a child where for everything someone does you say either "I made you do that" or "I knew you were going to do that"? I can really do it: Both know what you're going to do, like I knew you would shake your head that way, and make you do things, like I made you stand up then. I can do that so easy, sometimes I have to think afterward to know which I've done.

Before you go, would you let me have the tape recorder all the time? If I tell my story just three hours a week it will take more time than I can spare.

Pardon me, you did play the game with your brother Ralphie, right? See what I mean when I say it's better if I'm out of here? Becoming another rotten apple in a barrel is easier than you think.

2

THE FIRST I KNEW Mr. Peckham even existed was when I began my assignment on the men's ward. I won't say that was the worst day I can remember, but it was the seventeenth worst.

In the first thirty minutes it was obvious that the resident whose place I'd taken had obtained excessive gratification from the dependency needs of the patients. Over and over I heard how kind and understanding Dr. Phillips had been and shouldn't I get in touch with him before I changed any medicine. Then there was a mixup, and some wives showed up for a group therapy session I hadn't expected, which meant an hour of the morning spent listening to the same sort of thing from a chorus.

Somebody in that fan club must have sneaked in a bottle, because when I came out of the conference room three alcoholics were "high" and noisy. I tried to ignore them, but one kept saying in a voice you could hear all over the ward, "Don't be so stuck up, Doc. Have a drink with us."

When I did come over he said, "You'll have to find it first." I wasted fifteen minutes more looking through their things before I gave up and got back to work.

Then Mrs. Bailey saw me writing with my fountain pen.

"Will that write through?" She meant would the carbon copy show under the order sheet.

"Oh, yes," I said, but she took the chart and looked at it.

"It says here at the top, 'Use Ball-Point Pens Only.'"

"This is the only kind of pen I carry."

"We have plenty of pens at the desk."

"They don't even say 'please,'" I said. "Why should they tell me what kind of pen I can write with, and why don't they ask me? They are interfering with my rights. I know it's a little thing, but you give up little rights before you give up big ones, and why should I give up any? I don't like ball-point pens. They should spend more money on better carbon paper rather than tell me what I'm to write with."

Mrs. Bailey was watching me all this time and when I smiled, she did.

"Now what do I do?" I asked. "Make a stand for personal freedom or compromise and use a ball-point?"

Mrs. Bailey stopped smiling.

"I'll compromise," I said and went to get one of their throw-away pens.

This problem had come up often enough (three months ago the head nurse on the women's ward had told me the same thing without being so bossy), and long ago I'd learned to deal with it

3

by surreptitious resistance. When specifically asked or told to use a ball-point pen I would smile and say, "Oh, yes," as if I'd been writing with my own pen through absentmindedness.

There was nothing surreptitious about my stupid outburst, though. Now I'd get to use my pens far less than if I'd managed to keep my mouth shut, and now Mrs. Bailey would mention to the senior resident that Dr. Boyd seemed excitable.

I'd better explain; my attitude is not plain obstinacy: I'm a collector. I got started when I went with my mother once into a thrift shop and discovered in a bin of used fountain pens (it was when ball-points had become popular and everyone was intrigued with the idea of writing under water) a green Lifetime Sheaffer that had *Sanford Haworth* engraved on it. He had been the owner once, and I thought his name the most romantic I'd ever heard. In those days you could get a fine pen like that for fifty cents (now that everybody's on the bandwagon they are at least three dollars), and my mother bought it for me without arguing.

It was the beginning of a game that I added to when I could: first with more heroes, Richard M. Van Riper and Harley Mayfield and then villains, C. D. Brets and Leon F. Kysor and later the smaller ladies' pens to quarrel over, Nita McGovern, Lillian Sullivan, and the fairest of the fair, a robin's egg blue Conklin, Cynthia Bromwell.

They are so scarce now it's hard to believe that once I only bought those with names I liked.

When I finished on the open ward and started seeing the patients in the rooms, a nurse came along with me. It shows how preoccupied I was that I didn't notice her at first.

We came to a manic, obese man who was hypertensive and a diabetic and who looked like a child's drawing of a person with a dumpling body and pipestem arms and legs. This may be another one, I thought, for two months ago on the women's ward I'd discovered the first Cushing's syndrome I or most of the people in the hospital had ever seen or, rather, recognized. I looked through this man's chart and saw where steroid excretion studies

4

had been done and were normal. Dr. Phillips, the most loved man in the hospital, was bright too.

I about reached the conclusion, right then, that if there were any unusual patients on the ward he would have found them, but it turned out there was one, and I overlooked him too, for several days.

In one of the rooms was a twenty-three-year-old schizophrenic who had been rehospitalized after being outside for a couple of years. He was a good-looking, well-built young man with blond crew-cut hair that had grown out too long to be neat.

When he saw me he said, "I know you," and he paused as though trying to place me exactly. Then he smiled. "Of course, you're Jesus."

I've never worn a beard, but there is no accounting for the references of some psychotics.

He looked at the nurse and said, "And I know you too, you're Mary."

I caught a glimpse of dark hair, made-up eyes, and tanned skin that contrasted with her white uniform and then I looked quickly away.

She said, "No, I'm just a nurse," in a voice like a TV commercial I'd heard where a woman says, "No, I'm thirty-five."

Most people you can look at, but sometimes if they are very ugly or very beautiful, like this nurse, you can't, not at first anyway, without staring. By looking now and then back and forth across her, I could see she was tall and slim, that her legs and everything were as spectacular as her face, and on the second try I read her name tag: Mrs. Waggoner, R.N.

I thumbed through the chart and checked the medications the young man was getting and found that Dr. Phillips had done as well here as everywhere else. I couldn't find anything to change and was disappointed, because if I hadn't noticed Mrs. Waggoner till then I was sure she still hadn't noticed me.

My last patient, an Ernest Peckham, was in the end room on my side of the hall.

3

HE LAY VERY STILL with the head of the bed at a forty-five-degree angle, so that he seemed to be staring at the opposite wall.

"How do you do, Mr. Peckham," I said. He blinked his eyes, but there was no other sign that he had heard or that he knew anyone was there.

I looked through the thick chart. It began over a year ago, and that wasn't all, for the first entry said that an earlier part was stored in the record room. There were pages and pages of nurses' notes, and a few sheets of progress notes written by a succession of residents.

Perhaps if I hadn't been behind or if I had been having a better day, I would have recognized in the progress notes a clue to Mr. Peckham's secret, for they were all alike: "About the same." "Little change today." "Patient shows little change."

The sheet that had the information taken on his admission was a reproduction, and such a poor one that I had trouble reading it. He had come into the hospital—was readmitted, actually— eight years before, with a diagnosis of chronic deteriorated schizophrenia. According to the birthdate given, he would be fifty-five years old now.

I passed my hand in front of his eyes, but there was no response.

"Mr. Peckham, I am the new resident in charge of your case," I said, for often such people are very aware of their surroundings.

"I am taking care of you now," I said more loudly and distinctly.

"How are you feeling?" He only blinked his eyes.

6

He was a small man. I later weighed him several times, and always got 112 pounds or 50.80208 (Sorry, that's misleading; the scales aren't that accurate. I'm trying to stop that sort of computation and I have, except when I'm thinking about something else.) or 50.8 kilograms, and was five feet six and one-half inches tall, or rather long, because I never got a chance to measure him standing. The world Mr. Peckham had entered left fewer marks of the passage of time than the world of the people taking care of him, for he didn't look fifty-five. His hair was light brown, without any gray, and his face was unlined. There was a flakiness of the scalp and of the skin about his nose and chin. The pupils in the pale blue eyes reacted normally to light.

I slipped a tongue blade between the thin, barely pink lips and pushed down on the lower teeth. I had expected resistance, but his mouth opened easily. What I thought at first were dentures were not.

"Extraordinary," I said.

For the first time since Mrs. Waggoner had denied being Mary I was unaware of where she stood, what she was doing, or even that she was in the room.

"What's so extraordinary?" She was probably impatient, for I'd been trying to impress her with my thoroughness and was taking longer with my examinations.

"This might very well be the only fifty-five-year-old man in the world who has all his teeth, no fillings, and no cavities that I can see."

When I turned back to my patient, I was almost sure Mrs. Waggoner's eyes were brown.

Mr. Peckham's blood pressure was ninety-six over fifty-eight and his pulse was forty-eight. That these were so low I supposed was due to his state of virtual hibernation. I finished my examination without finding anything else as unusual as his remarkable teeth.

"Well, goodbye, Mr. Peckham," I said, "I will see you again soon." When I talk to patients who I don't expect will answer I unconsciously raise my voice, but I could have whispered or shouted. He only looked straight ahead and blinked his eyes.

7

I wrote "Condition seems stable" on the progress sheet. It was an entry I hadn't noticed on skipping through the chart.

I had read about patients like Mr. Peckham, but he was the first I'd seen. I knew though that once they had filled the back rooms of mental hospitals, where they lived out their days so encysted in their private worlds that no one could tell how much mind they might still possess. Most of them, the survivors of an era before psychotropic drugs, had been transferred to nursing homes, for they couldn't benefit from the attentions of psychiatric nurses, social workers, and psychiatrists. Why hadn't Mr. Peckham gone there?

Outside his room, I said, "On the chart it says that he was readmitted eight years ago, but it doesn't say how long he was out of the hospital, where he was, or how long he had been here before that."

Mrs. Waggoner said, "I don't know about his being out of the hospital then. I thought he'd been here longer than anyone, any of the patients or the staff."

"Well," I said, "I'll check over his old chart and see if he can't be transferred to a nursing home."

"That's what Dr. Phillips thought ought to be done."

I resolved then to show her that I was a man of action.

I thanked her for making rounds with me, and as she walked away I knew she was going to be a great delight to watch. But I knew, too, that I was going to think about her too much and lose sleep and lose weight, and people would say, "Who'd believe he could get thinner."

* * *

That night when the power went off, I came back over to the hospital and walked the dark and echoing halls to the personnel office. At first I looked for some tool to jimmy the door, but then, because there was no need for silence anywhere any more, I kicked out the glass and reached through and turned the knob.

Minutes later with her card in my pocket, I was out on the street looking for a car with the keys left in. I had never driven, but it's not much of a trick when you don't have to watch for anyone else.

The tricycle in the front yard meant at least one child and a difficult period of adjustment ahead, but I could wait. She awoke at once when I touched her bare shoulder.

"What in the world are you doing here?" She hadn't screamed; perhaps there had been a feeling there I hadn't recognized.

I stepped over to raise a window blind on the darkened city.

"I'm very much afraid," I said, "that we are the only two people left."

She accepted the fact at once. Questions as to what had happened could wait till tomorrow. Now she sensed how my eyes were held by the darker shadow of her nipples. They moved as she leaned back on an elbow.

"Well," she said, "there will be problems, and not the least is half of the time having to have intercourse in the dark, but we might as well get on with it."

4

MR. PECKHAM had two more days of the best care that can be given on a limited state budget before I got down to the record room to look at his old chart. It was four inches thick and began six years ago and even this wasn't all, for someone had written on the first page, "For the prior portion of this chart, see Microfilm #3484."

I began thumbing through it, and in five minutes was certain something was wrong and in fifteen minutes more I knew what it was. Except for the dates, the pages could have been in the chart upstairs.

What was wrong was simply that nothing had ever been wrong with Mr. Peckham, or rather nothing besides his primary illness. In over six years, he had never had a cold, diarrhea, a bed sore, or even an elevation of temperature. I was familiar enough with nurses' notes to know that they look for things to add variety to what they write and that in Mr. Peckham's case there simply hadn't been anything else to put down.

He went to physical therapy three times a week where his limbs were put through a full range of motion to prevent anky-losis and, on the days he didn't go there, he was taken in a wheel-chair and left in the day room for an hour or two. He had a bed bath twice a week. He always ate when fed, but sometimes he refused the last part of his meal. Every other day, he had passed what was recorded as a "moderate amount of formed stool" or "a well-formed stool." Regularly as each new psychotropic drug had been introduced, he had been given it in gradually increasing doses until someone somewhere reported toxicity at that level or a new drug became popular. And in all this time, if he had made a single voluntary motion or said a word, no one had recorded it.

I knew then, of course, that he was unusual, but I was thinking along lines of antibody titres and gamma globulin levels. A so-phisticated laboratory might track it down, I thought, but not ours here in the hospital, and besides I didn't have the time for it. Except that now I knew my patients' names, my work on the floor wasn't going much better than it had the first day.

There was another reason why I wanted to get on with his discharge. In the five years this part of the chart covered, three different residents had decided he should be transferred, and two of them had written orders sending him to specific nursing homes, but for some reason that wasn't clear, he hadn't gone. Mr. Peck-ham, I thought, must be a relative of some official with influence or maybe even the governor. If they were going to be so careful about hewing the line on the rules and make me use a ball-point pen, I wanted to see how they'd like hewing it all the way.

I went back to the floor, and on the way to the nurses' station passed Mrs. Waggoner and Dr. Shields, who were standing close together. They were deep in some conversation and ignored me, and I walked by briskly as though discharging Mr. Peckham after all these years was the most important thing that was going to happen in the hospital that day.

The nighttime fantasies about Mrs. Waggoner had started, and I'd already lost two pounds.

Should I confront her? "Mrs. Waggoner," I would say, "I am sorry to interrupt, but this is a matter of great urgency. Solely because of you one sixty-fifth of me is gone."

She would widen her mascaraed eyes in dismay, but Dr. Shields, of course, would say, "So why don't you try to lose the rest, Stevie boy?"

Her laugh then, how would it sound? It showed how lovesick I was that I almost turned back to find out.

At the nurses' station, I called a nursing home from a list they kept there. Mrs. Bailey heard me making the arrangements for the ambulance.

"Here is a pen to write the order with," she said and handed me a ball-point pen. "This place won't seem the same without Mr. Peckham."

"I can't imagine a patient who is benefiting less by being here," I said. "Why wasn't he transferred long ago?"

"Once, when we had medical students coming here, they used him for teaching. He was an example of what used to happen to schizophrenics. But that was a long time ago, and I don't know why he is still here now. Dr. Phillips mentioned moving him several times, but he never got around to it. He was *so* interested in psychotherapy." Evidently Mrs. Bailey had been another conquest of Dr. Phillips.

"Did you ever hear of Peckham Park?" she asked.

"No."

"It is a large park at the edge of the city with lots of trees, playgrounds, and a swimming pool," she said. "Mr. Peckham is one of those Peckhams."

I thought, well, just the same, he doesn't belong here.

"Does he ever have any visitors?"

"No, no one comes to see him, ever. Not that it would make any difference to him."

"Do you think he is still here because of family influence with some higher-ups?"

"Well, I guess we will find out," she said, but she wasn't as friendly as she had been. It was the wrong kind of question from a first-year resident after three days on the ward.

* * *

When the governor called and asked to talk to me, it would be Mrs. Waggoner who answered. She'd say, "Dr. Boyd, the governor is on the phone. It's our state governor; he wants to talk to you." She would be impressed; she would really look at me.

"Hello, Governor," or "Hello, Your Honor," where could I find out which was right? Mrs. Waggoner is watching; those beautifully made-up eyes are wide open.

"Dr. Boyd, there's a patient on your ward, he comes from a very influential family. They have made a lot of generous contributions to the city and the state."

"Not to mention some campaign fund contributions," I'd say. Then I'd wink at Mrs. Waggoner. "Just a sec, Governor," and I'd put my hand over the mouthpiece. "Would you listen on that other phone, dearie, I just might need a witness to this." She'd hurry to the other phone and pick it up and lean forward, and I found I could talk to the governor and look down the front of her uniform at the same time.

"You were saying, Governor."

"Well, be that as it may, they are a fine old family, pioneer stock, a family the state owes a debt to. The name, if you haven't guessed, is Peckham. Now, I understand that through an oversight or from overzealousness, you have discharged an Ernest Peckham. I wish you could see your way clear to make an exception to the prevailing rule that governs such discharges and keep him in the hospital."

"Governor, please let me quote to you the policy of the hospital in regard to patients such as Mr. Peckham." I'd have to look up that policy or rule so that I'd have it word for word. While I'm quoting it, I reach over and pat Mrs. Waggoner on the neck and side of the face, to reassure her, because she's nervous and worried for my welfare.

"Dr. Boyd, don't be difficult; as your governor, I'm not asking now, I'm ordering."

"Well, Gov, this is what you do. You get the administrator of the hospital to just rewrite that policy so that it excepts members of families who make campaign contributions, and I'll go along with that; otherwise, you will have to accept my resignation. But before you do, I wish you would check my qualifications and see if you think this hospital can afford to lose me. And one thing more, Gov. If I leave, at least one highly valued member of the staff will, I believe—" My eyebrows are raised; my look at Mrs. Waggoner is cool, appraising, inquiring. She nods eagerly "—will leave with me."

I take the hand that is not holding the phone, because that is how we will walk out, hand in hand.

"But take your time, Governor, I can hold up things on this end for twenty-four hours while you think it over."

*　*　*

"Stevie boy, I'll take that pen, if you're through."

It was Dr. Shields, who didn't mind ball-point pens, and when he had first seen one of my pens had asked, "Do you pump that up with a lever?"

He was a tall, Nordic, Van Riper type with blond hair that was longer than it was supposed to be and fair skin that, I thought, would let a lot of veins show through, sometime.

I saw patients in individual psychotherapy for the next two hours. It was an unpleasant chore and I couldn't decide whether I didn't like it because I wasn't good at it or whether it was the other way around.

I'd never been very effective at conducting group psychotherapy either, for that matter; some member was always taking over from me. So far I was best at family counseling, but it was only because they got so mad at me for some of my observations it brought them closer together, which is not the way it is supposed to work at all.

13

I was leaving the ward for the day when I saw two men in uniform wheel a stretcher down the hall for Mr. Peckham. Now that he was leaving without any fuss being made, I was kind of sorry I hadn't kept him awhile. I supposed then that I'd always wonder about the little man who'd tucked himself away in his mind.

5

THE NEXT DAY I made rounds alone, but the day after that Mrs. Waggoner was with me. She was wearing stockings, or what was more likely panty hose, with an intricate bright-colored diamond design that looked out of place with her nurse's uniform.

Once on "The Late Show" Jimmy Cagney had stepped back and really looked at a girl's legs and said, "Some gams."

I'd decided I'd do it—after all, the stockings invited comment—and was trying to pick the right time and getting more nervous from thinking about it when she said, "What an interesting pen."

I was carrying an anonymous one, jade green and similar to Sanford Haworth.

"Yes," I said, "it's an old Sheaffer. Do you want to look at it?"

"Why, it's beautiful," she said, but she kept her hands folded across the charts she was carrying. She wouldn't touch it.

I started telling her about pens, the old Parkers, Wahls, and Swans, et cetera, and how the old square-ender is fast disappearing, though very few people worry about it. But I stopped pretty soon because she looked over my shoulder and I wondered if she'd seen Dr. Shields and, let's face it, unless you're a pen enthusiast that's liable to be dull conversation. We'd broken the ice,

14

though; I was more determined than ever to say something about her legs.

When we got to the last patient and I hadn't managed it I decided I'd drop behind her as we walked back up the hall and say it there.

We came out the door and she started the wrong way. "Aren't you going to see Mr. Peckham?" she asked.

"I thought he'd gone to a nursing home."

"No, he's in here." Mrs. Waggoner opened the door and there was Mr. Peckham lying in his bed as he had been for years.

"There he is," she said.

"Some gams!" It was too loud; I'd startled her.

"What?"

I was looking directly at her legs, but perhaps it was a term she had never heard.

"Some gams—some gambulance attendants came for him; I saw them. I discharged him. I know I wrote the order." I tried to look cross as if that had been my reason for shouting.

"I don't know what happened," she said, "but I'll find out." And she left the room.

When she had been gone thirteen—a few sconds, Mr. Peckham said, "Hercules thirty-four," very distinctly.

I hadn't seen his lips move, hadn't even looked at him, but looked around me when the words came.

I did a stupid thing then, and it turned up later to plague me.

Lately I had been writing facetious notes on the charts now and then. For instance, a few days before, when the young man had called me Jesus and Mrs. Waggoner Mary I'd recorded it and added, "and believe me, a fellow couldn't ask for a nicer mother." I was sure no one read them and that it didn't matter what you put down as long as you wrote something twice a week.

Once I'd read a note written on a chart by a student nurse, "The patient passed a large amount of dark brown flatus," and I'd heard of a French entertainer who could enunciate a few words and play tunes by passing gas. I remembered how every other day for years Mr. Peckham's stools had been recorded and I wrote on the progress notes "Little change today except that the patient passed two well-formed words."

I expected that it would end up down in the record room with the rest of his chart and finally be microfilmed and kept forever without anyone seeing it, but this time I was wrong. Now even I have to agree it sounds like evidence of the anal fixation characteristic of paranoids.

While I waited for Mrs. Waggoner I took Mr. Peckham's pulse and blood pressure and got the same readings I had on the first day I'd seen him. Now I realized why in the chart that I'd studied there had been a slight variation in these findings while the temperature had always been ninety-eight degrees. They were simply less accurate determinations, and the results were more affected by the techniques of the persons obtaining them. Mr. Peckham's blood pressure and pulse had been as stable as his temperature.

Mrs. Waggoner came back, but she had been unable to find out what had happened. The ambulance attendants I had seen had come to get a patient of Dr. Shields, who also was leaving that day. The ambulance company insisted that Mrs. Bailey had called and canceled the ambulance. Mrs. Bailey said that she had not done that. In any case, another ambulance had been called and would be there some time that morning.

It was the most that Mrs. Waggoner had talked to me, and I listened to her voice, which I thought was beautiful though not quite so much so as it was sometimes when she talked to patients, and forgot to listen to what she said.

When her voice stopped, I had to say, "Pardon me, I was thinking of something else."

She gave me a funny look and explained it again, and this time I did pay attention, but she was a very distracting person.

Then I said, "I guess we had better cancel the ambulance because he has just said something."

"What was it?"

"'Hercules' and 'thirty-four.' It means something, probably a lot, to him. At any rate, the fact that he is talking means he is better. Let's get him up to the day room every day for a while. We can always send him away later."

I thought about saying, "Perhaps we should brush his hair to clear up that seborrhea," but if I said that she might do it herself, and the thought of lovely Mrs. Waggoner brushing dandruff from Mr. Peckham's scalp didn't seem right. And I wouldn't want her to be doing it and thinking, "I'm doing this because of that Dr. Boyd."

I don't know what would have happened if I hadn't canceled that ambulance, but I'm sure now that one way or another Mr. Peckham would still be right in that room.

6

DR. ENG, my senior resident, had the job of checking on the psychotherapy sessions I conducted with my patients. He was always very polite and very kind. He would go over the tape recordings with me and try to bolster my confidence but still point out mistakes I'd made and ways I could improve. I am sure there were times, though, when he wondered as I did if perhaps I was just not meant to be a psychiatrist.

My patients seemed to have fallen into two groups as far as their response to the sessions—or rather their behavior during the sessions—was concerned. There were some who wouldn't talk to me at all. Dr. Eng said that this was temporary, not to worry about it and that just to sit with someone was therapy, but these people gave no sign they were ever going to talk to me.

The silent ones were not as upsetting as those, the larger group, who had developed a negative transference (Dr. Shields calls this a fancy term for hating your guts) and talked all the time. When

Dr. Eng told me that this, too, was temporary and that they were acting out hostility meant for someone else, I understood perfectly and only wished he would explain it as well to the patients.

The young man who had said I was Jesus now thought that he was Pontius Pilate, which was certainly not progress.

One patient planned to "feed the world" and make himself a "millionaire multifold" by extracting maple syrup from the leaves of ordinary maple trees. He was sure I was "heading up" a group that was trying to get his secret from him, and was very quiet in his antagonism for me. I thought him capable of injuring me physically.

Then I overheard Mrs. Bailey say that she was going to have to get more help on the ward because there had never been so many incontinent patients and that it had been so much worse since Dr. Phillips had left. He was the one who had had my side of the ward before me and had written all the rosy progress notes on the people that I couldn't get to talk.

Except when she had a day off, there was always the compensation of watching Mrs. Waggoner, even though much of the time I was watching Mrs. Waggoner and Dr. Shields, for they seemed to have a lot to talk about.

Following the rule of always treating patients like people and not things, I talked to Mr. Peckham when I made rounds. I'd say, "How are you today, Mr. Peckham?" "I believe it's going to be another hot day today." "Could you tell me what you meant by 'Hercules thirty-four'?"

When Mrs. Waggoner wasn't with me, I'd say, "Isn't that a beautiful nurse who comes in with me sometimes?" or "I don't think you have noticed Mrs. Waggoner, but you really ought to— there can't be anything where you are that is quite like her."

There came a time when I was sorry I'd called his attention to her.

I made it a point to take his blood pressure and pulse every day and to always use the same blood pressure cuff, and whether he was sitting up in the day room or lying in his bed, the readings were always the same.

18

I had the next weekend off and I'd put the hospital and every-thing about it, except Mrs. Waggoner, out of my mind, when Sunday morning I saw in a newspaper headline the word Mr. Peckham had said. It seemed only a coincidence, but instead of skipping that part of the paper (it was in the financial section) as I usually did, I read the article.

The stock in a company by that name had been actively traded on the exchange the past few days and had had a phenomenal rise in price. An investigation had been promised because it had started up two days before the award of an important government contract.

I checked the dates again. When Mr. Peckham's message had come, the stock could have been bought at thirty-four. A day later, the flurry in trading had begun and the price had started up.

The combination of that particular date, a number, and an unusual word went beyond unlikely coincidence. The only ex-planation I could think of was that somehow Mr. Peckham had overheard the conversation of someone, perhaps a visitor to the day room, who had inside information about the market.

But I couldn't get the strange little man out of my mind, and finally I gave up reading the paper and went over to the hospital. I got the key to the medical library where it was kept at the in-formation desk and for the next three hours reviewed what a twelve-year-old physiology text (which isn't as bad as it sounds, for physiology doesn't change that much) had to say about blood pressure, pulse, and temperature.

I found a lot about what would increase or decrease all three but no clue as to what would cause absolute stability. I read about brain centers for control and neural pathways and receptor sites and when I'd finished, Mr. Peckham was more of a mystery than ever, for if he were as aware of his surroundings as I thought he was, this alone should have caused variations in his blood pressure and pulse.

On Monday, I went back to the record room and studied Mr. Peckham's old chart that had been stored on microfilm. His first admission was twenty-five years ago, when he had been trans-ferred from a private sanitarium, Harbor Hospital. I was disappointed with the description that I found of his childhood and of the initial stages of the illness, for it was much briefer than I'd hoped it would be. A resident years ago had decided that, since Mr. Peckham didn't talk, his case was not interesting enough to warrant taking a careful history. He could have done so, for Mr. Peckham's sister had brought him in and had been available to give any number of details that now when I talked to her (I'd decided that's what I must do) would be forgotten or inaccurately recalled.

She might have told the resident much more, but all that was on the chart was this: The date of his birth was given. His parents had been wealthy. He was exceptionally bright as a child but had not attended school (the reason for this was not given). Symptoms of childhood schizophrenia appeared at age five. By age twelve, he was totally withdrawn, and there had been no remissions and very little change in him since then. When he was fifteen, his parents were killed in an accident (no details were given), and he had been kept in the sanitarium until coming here.

Eight years ago, he was transferred to a nursing home called The Merri Hours, but in five days he was back in the hospital again. A note said only that he had been unmanageable in The Merri Hours.

Mr. Peckham unmanageable! I thought about that for a moment before I went on. It could only mean combative or noisy. I would have to find out more about his stay at Merri Hours, too.

And there was something else that made me wonder about his few days outside the hospital. He had not always had the blood pressure and pulse he had now and that the nurses had been entering on his chart twice a week for years. Before he had gone to the nursing home, these findings had been just as consistent, but slightly higher.

What had happened at the Merri Hours that had caused the change? But, I told myself, it wasn't the difference that was remarkable; that much variation could be found in many people even on consecutive days. It was the invariable stability before and after that was unnatural. Mr. Peckham's body had been set to function at a definite rate and, as we might carelessly push down a thermostat when we leave on vacation, it hadn't always been set at the same level.

The rest of the chart was much the same as what I had already seen. He never had an elevation of temperature, and I guessed that the three times it had been below normal, the thermometer had not been left in long enough. There was no mention of his speaking. Some of the residents had written progress notes in handwriting almost impossible to read, but when I deciphered it I found they agreed: Mr. Peckham had always been "about the same."

The only lab work in the chart was a routine blood count and urinalysis done on his first admission and repeated when he had been readmitted after being in the nursing home. Though there was an interval of seventeen years between the determinations, the results were identical.

I gave the role of microfilm back to the girl who had found it for me and went back up to the floor. At the nurses' station, there was a list of tests the hospital laboratory could do. I ordered all of them on Mr. Peckham.

7

MY OTHER INTEREST was Mrs. Waggoner, and she had no chart I could study. What was her first name? Why didn't she wear a ring? Did she have children? Where had she grown up and gone to school? Where did she live?

The first of these questions I most wanted answered and had

the least right to ask. The others might be asked casually, I thought, but there was no need to know her first name unless I intended to use it and, since that was impossible in the professional setting of the hospital, asking meant I wanted to use it elsewhere.

I could hardly say, "I must know your first name, it has become a necessary part of incantations I perform at night." It was true, though, "Mrs. Waggoner" had been too formal for some time and Cynthia was a poor substitute. I needed the real name.

I planned the question, where I would ask it (I had decided on Mr. Peckham's room, because there we were alone or at least seemed alone), and what I would say. I rejected, "I once knew a girl by the name of Cynthia Waggoner," and "I knew a family in California whose name was Wagner. Odd, but every generation had a Cynthia Wagner" because these would be as hard to say and might get me no answer at all and settled on, "What is your first name?"

But the planning was my undoing, for as we moved down the hall and came closer to Mr. Peckham's room I'd get in such a nervous state I couldn't trust my voice.

Perhaps, I thought, if I try to ask her and strangle on the words I should have a card to hand her saying, "I am not a diabetic and I am not having a seizure; I am having a laryngeal spasm from the question 'What is your first name?' "

I learned it finally without asking. There are rows of cards with employees' names by a time clock on the first floor. After several stops there while I pretended to set my watch, I saw her card: Grace Waggoner, R.N. It suited her, I thought.

She walked as though she had carried baskets on her head or, if she wore a long skirt like those I'd seen in *Gone with the Wind*, she'd glide as those women had, as if she were on roller skates.

There was no relief for me, though. When I'd read the card I became preoccupied with the next question, about the rings.

I'd made a definite decision one morning on "I don't see why they don't put plain 'Ms.' on those tags," and the tension had started up when I was given a reprieve by Mrs. Bailey, who called me away from rounds for a talk. She was in a bad mood and told me I would have to do something about one of my patients who had been here two months and never caused any trouble before but now had become combative. It turned out she was talking about the young man who thought Mrs. Waggoner was Mary. Yesterday in the day room, he had tried to attack Mr. Peckham.

I was given a firsthand account by an orderly who had been present. The young schizophrenic "had got it in his head" that Mr. Peckham was blinking his eyes at him.

"Maybe Ernie," the orderly called all the patients by their first names, "knows more about what goes on here than we give him credit for because it was just like Rog (the young man) was telling him when to blink. 'Now he's going to do it! Now he's going to do it!' Rog would yell, and sure enough, Ernie would blink. Well, I was going to take Ernie back to his room, 'cause even if he hadn't been there long enough I knew the situation was deteriorating."

The orderly paused for me to tell him he had done the right thing, and I assured him he had. "Then Rog shouts, 'If you won't make him stop, I will,' and he charges for him like he was going to run right over Ernie. He would of, too, 'cause I couldn't have stopped him; a deranged mentality makes some people quick as cats; but before he got to Ernie he slipped and fell. When he got up he'd forgot all about it and went off and started helping on a jigsaw puzzle. I took Ernie to his room, and when I came back I asked Rog if he was hurt. He says, 'God's finger touched me.' I guess he didn't get hurt 'cause I couldn't get him to say anything else."

While I finished rounds (I was by myself, for Mrs. Waggoner was busy with other duties) I thought more about yesterday's episode in the day room than about the patients I was seeing. What the young man had said about God's finger was to be expected, for he made many religious references. How had he known, though, when Mr. Peckham would blink? That he had somehow known, I was sure, for Mr. Peckham had never paid the slightest attention to me and I doubted that he had taken directions or obeyed commands from the young man.

23

In the room at the end of the hall after I'd watched Mr. Peckham's eyes for a few minutes, I used my wrist watch to time the interval between each blink. That was the answer; it was always forty seconds.

The young man may not have recognized this regularity, but it had enabled him to predict each lid movement. Except for him and his typical schizophrenic response, a bizarre feature of Mr. Peckham would have gone unnoticed.

After that, I went to the medical library again and read about blinking. Some of this I already knew, but I'll summarize it all here. Eye-blinking serves a purpose; it spreads tears over the eye; the cornea would dry out and ulcerate otherwise, because it has no blood supply. The contraction of the muscle, the *orbicularis oculi*, squeezes tears from the tear gland, and the closing lid spreads these over the eye. In a few diseases eye-blinking is infrequent; an example is hyperthyroidism. But nowhere could I find a reference to an exactly equal interval of the eye-blink, and nowhere could I find where anyone had even checked it.

There was no doubt about it. A regular EBI (eye-blink interval) was a new finding, one more entry to go under "signs" in Dorland's *Medical Dictionary* and if I could somehow learn what it signified I'd achieve immortality there between Boyce, who once heard a gurgling sound when pressing on the neck of a patient with a diverticulum of the esophagus, and Bozzolo, who noticed that the blood vessels of the nostrils pulsated when there was an aneurysm of the thoracic aorta.

On different occasions, I measured Mr. Peckham's EBI, first with my wrist watch and later with a stop watch. I timed as many as a hundred intervals and always got the same figure, about 39.75 seconds, for each one. I spent so much time in that room trying to find some variation in his EBI that I began to neglect my other work. Later I learned that the finest clocks (or for that matter the Greenwich Observatory) were not as accurate as Mr. Peckham, who lay there alone and blinked his eyes with an absolute and even astronomical exactness every 39.7532871+ seconds.

8

LIKE THE FIRST message, the second had a quality that made me involuntarily look around for the source. It was not loud, but still it was clear and distinct and so resonant that it set up brief echoes in the room. Again there was a single word and a number, this time "Stern forty-two."

I didn't bother to take his pulse or blood pressure or time his EBI (I was still trying then to measure his EBI with a wrist watch) but went straight downstairs and bought a paper. The stocks listed on the exchange have their names so abbreviated that they are hard to identify, but after fifteen minutes of study I was sure there was no Stern Company.

The "messages," after all, were in a private code of Mr. Peckham's. Where he was it was the only language thought or spoken; for me or anyone else it was nonsense.

Three days later I learned from a conversation going on at the residents' table that there might be such a company after all. There were other exchanges besides the one whose quotations I'd been looking at in the paper, and a lot of stocks weren't listed anywhere. That afternoon I called a stockbroker I'd looked up in the phone book. I was put through to a man who had a confident voice but sounded too young for such an important job.

"Would you recommend buying Stern at forty-two?" I asked.

The young man answered, "Well, you certainly should have a couple of days ago. You would have to pay fifty-seven for it now, and frankly we think it's a bit overpriced. We don't quite understand what's happened to that stock in the past few days." Then he went on, "If you would give me your name and address I'll see that you get a brochure with a list of stocks that we recommend as excellent buys right now, considering the state of the market."

I thanked him and said that I thought I knew where I could get the same information, and hung up.

Some of the lab work I'd ordered had started to come back. It was easy to see why Mr. Peckham had escaped detection for so long and why now even I who'd found him out didn't know what I'd found. Everything was either normal or in the low-normal range. Thyroid function was relatively lower than the other findings, but this was consistent with his near dormant state. Blood counts and urinalyses done in the past week agreed with those done years ago, as though they had been different determinations on the same specimens.

I found that getting all of this in the hospital laboratory, where usually there weren't many requests for lab work, wasn't always easy. Finally, when I wanted Mr. Peckham's stools analyzed, the lab people flatly refused. Every other day I'd sent them a stool, and after the third one without a report coming back I went to the lab to ask about the results. The technicians told me that it would be much simpler for me to flush them down the toilet in the ward, for that was what they had done and were going to continue doing in the lab. They didn't like it much better having me messing around in their lab (once I heard someone call me the hospital's new turd inspector), but I checked the stools myself, then. I was glad I'd done it too, for right away I found something amazing. The specimens were normal feces, but each weighed exactly 184 grams.

The electroencephalogram was a disappointment to me. Dr. Popper, the staff neurologist, made the notation, "unusual form of electrical interference. Impossible to interpret. Please repeat." The second tracing looked the same to me, and this time the note said only "Please repeat." Later on I gave up on electroencephalography as a help in finding out about Mr. Peckham. It's truly an empiric science. We know from examining thousands of tracings that many abnormalities cause specific changes but we don't know why. When a tracing was absolutely unique, Dr. Popper was lost and would be till the unlikely time someone published a series titled "Unusual EEG Characteristic of the Telepath."

9

MRS. WAGGONER must have wondered what was the matter with the skinny little resident who carried a different pen every day and whose voice got higher and shakier as he moved up the hall on his rounds. I'd rejected the statement about "Ms." after almost getting it out because I thought it would be my luck for her merely to agree with me. She might even think that was the safest thing to do when someone seemed so agitated.

Finally, one morning at the last minute before we left Mr. Peckham I blurted out, "Your tag says 'Mrs.,' but it doesn't say why you're not wearing rings."

She looked at me gravely for a moment. Perhaps she was wondering how small the print would have to be in order to get the whole story of an unhappy marriage along with her name on that tag.

"We have separated," she said.

It was an answer I'd heard in fantasy. Then she had added, "and I get so lonesome sometimes," in a voice so thoroughly miserable I had taken her arm. We had walked together then toward the big open ward at the end of the hall. Without speaking we shared the realization that now she was leaving her loneliness behind.

We did walk down the hall together, and I was ready to take her arm, but there was no signal from her.

That she had become accustomed to my stammering and false starts on questions was the reason, I suppose, why she did not suspect I was hearing voices when the morning came that I did.

It was Mr. Peckham's third message, and it arrived two days after I'd managed to ask about her rings.

On our way up the hall I'd been considering how to find out if she had children. The hospital was so free of the influence of children that it was a hard subject to approach unless I remarked on that fact and elaborated on how the hospital would be much more like life outside if we had children present and perhaps, for therapeutic reasons, staff members should be encouraged to bring their children to the hospital while they were on duty. It would have been a stupid remark, but the one I used was not much better.

"Don't you think he looks as helpless as a child?" I said when we came into Mr. Peckham's room.

"I never thought of that," Mrs. Waggoner said. "I can't imagine him as a child."

She stepped across and opened the window wider, and it was then that Mr. Peckham said "Eagle thirty-six" as certainly as he had "said" anything. The words were perfectly distinct, and there was the same persistent echoing quality.

"Except that voice, of course," I said, "there is nothing child-like about that."

"I wouldn't know." She turned back, "I've never heard him say anything."

And if she had, I was sure she couldn't have gone on raising the window.

What had happened then? I tried to think of explanations besides the one I wouldn't acknowledge yet. Had I heard them myself? The sound had been all around me a few seconds ago. Had there been some trick of acoustics that blanked out part of the room? No, it had been everywhere. And, still not examining what was waiting in my mind and would have to be faced, I wondered, had this been going on from the first? If it happened once it probably had before and would again.

What should I do now? Do everything as usual; there would be time later when we could examine this by degrees. A small part of me seemed to have gained a lot of influence simply because it had remained calm.

10

PERHAPS it was that I tried, for once, to concentrate on my work but I had, actually, a better day than usual, and even went through a group therapy session without one of the members taking over from me. Except for a brief period during a conversation at the lunch table, my denial of the experience at the end of the hall was complete.

The residents were on one of their favorite subjects, their "portfolios." They were arguing about what was going to go up and should be bought and what would go down or not go anywhere and should be sold.

During a lull in the conversation I said, probably too loudly because everybody stopped and looked at me, "I have a good tip: Buy Eagle at thirty-six."

Dr. Shields, who put ketchup on absolutely everything I ever saw him eat, stopped pouring.

"Stevie boy, where did you get that tip?"

"Never mind where," I said, "it's an unimpeachable source," which was true enough.

Maybe because I'd never talked much at the residents' table (I'm not a good "mixer," and more important, I didn't own any stocks), or because almost always when someone asked me about medicine I had what turned out to be the right answer, or for both reasons, several of the fellows took my tip. Dr. Jacobs and

Dr. Shields and several others bought Eagle, which was at thirty-six that day. I heard later that some others would have bought it, but their brokers talked them out of it.

That evening when I'd gone up to my room I turned the TV set on and then before it warmed up turned it off again. It was time to think about what had happened and what should be done.

I began with what I thought then was the worst possibility, that I was psychotic. Even in medical school I had recognized that I had the introverted personality of the potential schizophrenic. Was this the onset? Hallucinating as an isolated symptom was not enough to warrant the diagnosis, or so I'd been taught. What other evidence was there?

I'd been ineffective in my work, it was true, but that wasn't new. Long ago I'd accepted the possibility that because of my ineptness I might not be asked to continue my residency after my first year.

I hadn't exhibited bizarre behavior that I could think of. I wasn't depressed and I wasn't anxious either, except of course in the presence of Mrs. Waggoner. It was true that I was somewhat obsessive in my search for fountain pens, but I'd been that way for years.

No, I told myself, and I thought I was being objective, there is not enough evidence yet to warrant the diagnosis, even though it can't be ruled out, either.

I was glad to proceed to other possibilities: true paranoia—I was too young and hallucinations are rare in this condition; a toxic psychosis—I'd not been exposed to toxins, I was sure; a manic-depressive psychosis—though hallucinations could occur, I'd had no change in affect at all.

The second major possibility was that this had not been a hallucination but was telepathy and that I was the only person who had or could receive the messages. I would not have guessed that reception would have simulated ordinary auditory reception so closely, but after all, speaking is how immediate thoughts are usually transmitted. We only read what has been thought by someone at some time in the past. There was no doubt that Mr. Peckham was extraordinary; the day before I had twice timed thirty EBIs, and the figures I'd gotten had agreed to a tenth of a second. After all, could there be anything much more extraordinary than that? I'd probably known all along I was going to arrive at this conclusion and call it tentative and tell myself I'd await developments that would either prove it or thoroughly convince me I was psychotic.

I've made a decision, I told myself then, and there's nothing gained in mulling it over, but now and then during the rest of the evening I thought of additional reasons why I'd been right. Psychotic people whom I'd heard describe their hallucinations always had had a source for them: a clothes closet, a television set, or even their ear, but never from all about them at once. Schizophrenics, especially at the onset of their illness, had frightening dreams; my dreams, when I dreamed at all, had been of Mrs. Waggoner and very pleasant.

That night, after I'd fallen asleep, I was summoned back to the ward by a telephone call. It was Mrs. Bailey, and she was angry.

Before the elevator got to the floor I heard a continuous rumble and irregular, high-pitched shouting. The ward was swarming with children of all ages from less than a year to late adolesence and all of them, even the crawling babies, were engaged in frenzied destruction of the place.

I made my way around tipped-over beds and stepped over an infant who clumsily tried to stab my leg with a broken thermometer. Dr. Shields, Mrs. Waggoner, and Mrs. Bailey with some aides and orderlies had barricaded themselves in the nurses' station. A bed on its side blocked the entrance and they moved it enough to let me in and then pulled it back again.

"It's your crackpot scheme," Mrs. Bailey said. "They got crazier than the grownups, and they are more active."

An emesis basin sailed by our heads and broke a window behind us.

"Let's try to get out," Dr. Shields said. "We aren't doing any good here."

"I won't leave without Leon," Mrs. Waggoner said. "He's got a thermometer and may hurt himself."

31

The din lessened, for there was nothing left to demolish and the mob began forming a ring around the station.

As we were forced back by the bed tipping over and the wild children surging over it, I woke up.

I got up and washed my face in cold water to keep from falling into my dream again. I hoped there wasn't going to be much of that sort of thing.

11

DR. FREUD BELIEVED in telepathy; psychiatrists today seriously discuss it and have published articles on the subject, but lay people still do not consider it a respectable topic for conversation. I couldn't, for instance, call Mr. Peckham's sister and ask, "Did you ever receive telepathic messages from your brother?" even though that was exactly what I had to find out.

I planned an indirect approach. I'd introduce myself as the doctor taking care of her brother. She might apologize for not coming to see him oftener and I'd say, "Oh well, I suppose you keep in touch." If that didn't get results I'd say, "He's communicating with me," and give her time to make some comment. Finally I might say, "It's been in a very unusual way," but without some sign from her that she understood I couldn't go much farther than that.

If she hadn't received telepathic messages or hadn't recognized them, I still wanted to ask questions about their childhood. Did he always find her when they played hide-and-seek? Did he always somehow seem to get his way? Had someone miraculously intervened in time of trouble?

And if I drew a blank on everything (she might have decided

long ago never to tell anyone about her brother's ability), I still had to have her permission to see Mr. Peckham's old chart from Harbor Hospital.

Nothing went the way I'd planned. There was a long wait while the woman who'd answered the phone went somewhere after Mrs. Vukov. When she came on the line I introduced myself and she whispered, "Who is it?"

I told her who I was again and she whispered, "Now tell me who you really are."

I had the feeling it was a conversation I'd had somewhere before, and then realized it was just that she sounded so paranoid.

Finally she said, "If you're taking care of my brother, why are you calling here?"

"If you'd tell me something about him it will help me."

"His name is Ernest Peckham and he's fifty-five years old," she was whispering again. "See, it didn't help at all."

"Did he talk much as a child?" I asked.

"Did he talk as a child? He talked as a baby. He didn't talk like a baby. He didn't talk like a child either. No, he didn't talk much as a child, but he talked more than he does now. Ernest doesn't talk at all now. Maybe he doesn't talk because people are listening like people are listening now."

"Mr. Peckham has begun to communicate with me," I said.

She said without whispering, "How is he doing that?"

I made a mistake then, I suppose because of the training here to invariably be honest with psychotic patients. Before I thought I'd said, "By telepathy, of course."

She didn't answer and I asked, "Did you ever receive messages from him?"

She said again, "Are you really one of the doctors at the hospital?"

I said that I was. She wouldn't believe me and asked who I really was.

I asked to speak to her husband since even if I couldn't find out anything of Mr. Peckham I needed that authorization to see his chart.

"You know very well he is in Europe," she said.

"I don't know your husband," I said, "and I am a doctor at the hospital."

"I would like to believe you," she said. Then the first woman spoke and I realized she had been listening to the whole conversation.

"I think there has been about enough of this. Hang up the phone, Mrs. Vukov."

Mrs. Vukov said, in a normal voice, "Dr. Boyd, if you leave your number perhaps I can call you back. However, they keep me a prisoner here and eavesdrop on my every conversation."

I heard one phone hang up then and guessed that Mrs. Vukov's attendant would soon interrupt the call, and that's what happened.

"Never mind about Ernest," she said, "he will manage. You better take care of yourself," and the line went dead.

I hadn't learned anything about her brother or gotten permission to see the old chart. And somewhere a stranger, probably a practical nurse, knew that a person who called himself Dr. Boyd was hearing voices. If I made many slips like that I'd never find out about Mr. Peckham.

I decided then to go out to the sanitarium, introduce myself as Mr. Peckham's doctor, and ask to see his old chart. Psychiatric institutions are very careful about who they show their records to, but if I acted confident enough I might get to see it. Also some employees might still be there who remembered him, and though I would have to be more careful than I had been with Mrs. Vukov I wanted, at least, to see their reaction when I mentioned his name.

Most people undertaking a trip like that (Harbor Hospital is at the city limits on the north side of town) would have left work an hour early and driven out and taken care of it in an afternoon, but it wasn't that easy for me. I don't own a car, don't even know how to drive. Generally I'd gotten along very well, but now a car would have been a great time-saver.

It would be several days before I would have time off during the week. In the meantime I hoped no one would call the sanitarium and warn them I might be coming.

12

THE NEXT MONDAY noon, there was excitement at the lunch table. The residents had gotten the latest stock quotations from a television set somewhere in the hospital. Eagle Industries was at forty-three. Those who hadn't followed my advice wanted to know if it was too late to buy, and the ones who had, wanted to know if now they should sell. Someone else wanted me to find out if he ought to sell some oil stock he owned.

"I only get calls now and then," I said, "when my informant knows something for sure. I have to wait for a message from him, and he never seems to want to talk very long or answer questions."

They had asked before and now someone asked again, "Can't you tell us where you got the tip?"

"No," I said, "if I did there would be serious repercussions for someone," which was true enough.

Dr. Shields said, "Well, never mind where it came from. Just tell me when you decide to sell your Eagle stock. That will be good enough for me."

"I didn't buy any," I said.

"You didn't buy any?" Dr. Shields asked.

The talk quieted down then because Dr. Hahn had brought his tray to our table.

Dr. Shields said, "Dr. Hahn, I want to thank you for recommending bromides for that manic I asked you about. It really makes a lot of difference."

Dr. Hahn had been a psychiatrist when they called them alienists and when bromides were one of their main remedies. I was

35

surprised the pharmacy had any in stock; it was medicine that dated from the era of using leeches and raising blisters.

Dr. Hahn said, "Well, sometimes the old tried-and-true approach is the best. Bromides will be around when some of these new phenothiazine drugs are forgotten."

I was sure Dr. Shields hadn't given anyone bromides and that later in the afternoon Mrs. Waggoner and he would be laughing over the conversation.

Dr. Hahn said, "What were you fellows talking about when I came to the table?"

Dr. Shields said, "Stevie—I mean Dr. Boyd—has just been giving us some tips on the stock market."

"I thought you might have been having a clinical discussion," Dr. Hahn said. "There is plenty of time for you to reap financial rewards when you get into practice. I think it is far better while you are here learning your profession to confine your interests to medicine and to helping the patients. A too-early interest in materialistic things does not speak well for your motivations in becoming a doctor. If you concentrate on increasing your clinical ability now, you will be more than amply rewarded, financially, later on. Believe me, I speak from experience."

I said, "Yes, sir," but I thought about saying, "Yes, sir, and if you look like a Jewish Dr. Gillespie and you're a good politician you might get to be chief of staff of a state hospital and then you're rewarded for practically nothing." If I'd said it, there would have been at least three people there aspirate their food. Maybe I could anticipate that and do multiple emergency tracheotomies and become a hero.

Then to more or less prove his point, I suppose, Dr. Hahn started talking about a trip he had made to the Far East, including Japan and Hong Kong. He invited us all to come to see his slides the next Friday at his home.

Dr. Shields asked about bringing "a young lady." I knew who that would be and that she wouldn't be wearing a uniform, either. Next Friday night, no matter what, I was going to be at that slide show.

Though the residents asked every lunch hour (for a while they were even stopping by my room after work) I didn't pass on any more tips.

There was another message the next day, and for the second time in a row Mrs. Waggoner was there when it arrived. We came into the room and she stepped over to raise the window as she usually did.

"It always seems so stuffy in here," she said.

I still didn't know if she had any children and was as close to asking as I'd ever been when she began a conversation.

"Why do you always take his blood pressure and pulse?"

"It's always exactly the same," I said.

"If it's always the same, why do you need to take it?"

"Because of that," I said. "I've never seen a patient before whose blood pressure and pulse never varied. And the lab work, I've gotten all sorts of lab work and repeated it and it's always the same. Don't you think that is interesting?"

"No," she said, "I don't think he is any more interesting than a parsnip and a lot more repulsive. If there were many patients like him I'd go into another kind of nursing."

At last we were having a real conversation like those she had so often with Dr. Shields, and I wanted it to continue.

I told her about the EBI that was so regular I hadn't been able to figure out how regular it actually was, but I'd gotten flustered and forgot to tell her what EBI stood for. "And every bowel movement weighs 184 grams," I said. "Can you imagine that? Normal people don't have stools that always weigh the same. Yours and mine don't."

She didn't say anything but from the look she gave me I guessed she was thinking, "And if all psychiatrists were like you I'd go into some other kind of nursing, too."

Before we left the room, the word "unicorn" and the number "thirty-nine" were as plain and unmistakable as the others had been. Mrs. Waggoner walked through it as though there was nothing there.

At lunch when the residents asked me what news I had of the market, I said, "Well, I do have a tip, but financial rewards come

37

very soon after you get into practice. I think we ought to confine our interest now to the wealth of clinical material available to us."

Dr. Shields said, "Stevie, I want to apologize about that, but once he had started I couldn't very well stop him and tell him I was the mercenary bastard, and anyway he wouldn't have believed it if I had."

What he said was probably true, but Dr. Hahn had given us good advice and I told them so.

I never passed on any more tips, and because I didn't, and didn't invest myself, they stopped coming.

13

I HAD A THEORY then about what was happening. In the day room, there were always newspapers. Mr. Peckham had seen enough of these, plus what he might have overheard people saying, so that, in the almost limitless time he had at his disposal, he had been able to devise a formula that worked at least part of the time on the stock market. It was no stranger than what idiot savants could do. I'd never seen one but I'd read how they could give immediate answers to impossible problems dealing with the calendar.

The telepathy was a freakish hypertrophy of an ability (I'd always doubted reports of telepathy but I welcomed them now) many people had.

I had left then to explain the unchanging physical findings and lab tests. I began ordering work from a private laboratory that would be more accurate and where I could get more things done.

If I believed my rationalizations completely, why did I keep the messages a secret? I was gathering evidence, I told myself, that would absolutely prove what an extraordinary creature I'd found.

There was another answer that I began to refute again and again, though I recognized that the form my refutations took was a symptom and tried to stop: Dr. Shields and Mrs. Waggoner are talking; if I were psychotic I'd think it was about me. Mrs. Bailey's writing a note; I know it doesn't concern me, so I'm well. The residents were talking about their stocks while I was in the cafeteria line; they are quiet now because Dr. Hahn's come into the room, not because I've just sat down. A crazy person wouldn't be that sensible.

I didn't wait for my day off to go out to Harbor Hospital, but told Mrs. Bailey and Dr. Eng I had some business in the city that couldn't wait and made the trip on Wednesday.

After I got to the bus terminal, I called the city bus company to find out what local bus to take. A lady on the phone told me I wanted a No. 39 and where to catch it.

"How high do your buses go?" I asked.

"How high do they go?"

"What is the highest number on your buses?" I asked again.

"Fifty-three."

"Do you have a bus for every number?"

"Those are lines, not buses, and we don't have a line for every number."

"How many lines do you have?"

But she had decided I was wasting her time and had hung up.

I had told the driver where I wanted off, but when I saw it I knew I couldn't have missed it. We had been traveling through block after block of nearly identical houses, all white frame in Cape Cod style and all on city-sized lots, and right in the middle of this was a long, two-story building surrounded by several acres of old orchard. I got off the bus and had gone only a few feet up the driveway when the big cherry trees blocked out the development houses of the normal people and I felt I'd come back to the world of the odd ones.

Harbor Hospital was a Victorian house that had had wings added on the sides long after the gingerbread in the middle had gone out of style. I rang the bell and a very obese lady in a nurse's uniform let me in. On her name tag I saw "Mrs. Hall" and below that "Head Nurse."

I introduced myself and began telling her about Mr. Peckham, who had been a patient there twenty-five years ago, but she interrupted me. She had only been there five years and would know nothing about him, but I could talk to Mrs. Kappleman, who owned the hospital and had owned it then. She led me to an office that must have been the den in the original old house.

Mrs. Kappleman was sixty or perhaps even older and was such an attractive woman I felt disappointed that I'd never seen her in her twenties, for then she must have been almost, or perhaps completely, beautiful. She had a southern accent and a natural grace that made me feel clumsy.

I introduced myself again and asked if she remembered a Mr. Peckham, who had been a patient there twenty-five years ago.

"Ernest Peckham; of course I remember Ernest," she said. "He was a member of the Peckham family."

Then an aide brought in her lunch and she asked if I had eaten yet. When I said I had not, she began making room on her big walnut desk for a second tray. Among the things that were pushed aside was an empty bottle that had held one thousand Empirin tablets, and because it was so large everything about it was large: the label and the manufacturer's trademark, a prancing unicorn. I was relieved; I'd been watching for it ever since I'd learned the number of the bus.

When I sat down across from her, she turned the bottle so the label faced me directly, and said, "I can't throw this away or else I'll forget to order more."

The food was very good, much better than in our cafeteria.

But now instead of telling me about Mr. Peckham, she asked me questions about myself and told me about the hospital as though the meal had made it a social occasion, and now it was not genteel to immediately talk of my main reason for coming.

The hospital had been the country home of a wealthy pioneer family who had a city street and an office building named after them. Once that whole area had been their farm and the fruit trees outside were their orchard. The house had been added to over the years, but the entrance—in fact, the whole middle of the building—was part of the original house and over eighty years old.

She had bought the hospital twenty-eight years ago and Mr. Peckham was one of the twenty patients who were there then. His doctor was Dr. Adler, and she asked if I knew him (I didn't then). He was still in practice and still had an occasional patient at Harbor. She was surprised to hear that Ernest was talking and didn't believe he ever had since the fire. By "the fire" she meant when the Peckham home had burned and Ernest's parents hadn't been able to get out so that all that was left of that family was a sister who hadn't been home and Ernest, whom you really couldn't count, for in a sense he hadn't been a member of the family even before the fire.

Mrs. Kappleman stopped for a moment and poured us more coffee. "How did Mr. Peckham get out of the fire?" I asked.

"I don't know," Mrs. Kappleman said. "I don't know if I ever knew all the details. That was forty years ago."

"Why did he leave, or I mean, why was he transferred?"

"The family, or, rather, Mrs. Vukov, his sister—did you know she has been a patient here, too?"

"What was the matter with her?" I asked.

"She was schizoid, too, but nowhere near as bad as her brother. There were times when she was almost all right.

"Well, Mrs. Vukov," she continued, "would have been happy to have kept him here. That was before she was ever a patient here herself, not that that would have made any difference. But I had to ask her to move him."

For dessert there was apple pie with ice cream, but I forgot it was there. It was obvious that she thought she had finished telling me about Ernest and now was telling me of the problems she had with the employees.

And she had trouble with the employees, not the nurses—they were competent—but the aides and especially the orderlies, who often enough were borderline mental cases themselves. No one who was capable or normal would take such a job in the first place, and when you had found one who was fairly bright and not too obviously homosexual, as many orderlies were, you liked to keep them. Samuel Holden was an orderly who had learned quickly and become so necessary to the smooth running of the hospital and seemed so normal she had wondered why he was an orderly at all. So it had been a shock to her when one day he had asked to speak to her and then, right here in this office, told her, though he of course didn't call it that, of a delusion he had about Ernest. He believed Ernest could hypnotize him and make him do things. If he were late putting Ernest on the commode or giving him a urinal he would have to stop whatever he was doing and go take care of him. The only way he could avoid being forced like a robot to run errands for Ernest was to follow Ernest's schedule. Two days before, the patients had been outside when it started to rain. He'd been on his way to get them, including Ernest, who was in his wheelchair—even then he never walked—but he wanted to stop for his raincoat and found he couldn't. He had to walk right by the coat and get Ernest in before he could do anything else, and that was when he had decided to talk to Mrs. Kappleman.

Mrs. Kappleman was to decide then who would go, he or Ernest, because he would quit if she kept Ernest.

But it turned out not quite so simply as that, for Samuel had talked to some of the other help and soon she was faced with what she labeled (incorrectly) mass hysteria. If Ernest weren't transferred, three aides and a practical nurse would leave too and all for the same reason, so she had him transferred, even though no one paid their bills more promptly than the Vukovs, who paid for Ernest.

By then my ice cream had melted and run onto my tray.

"Where is Mr. Holden now?" I asked.

"He didn't work here more than six weeks after that," she said.

"How about the others: the practical nurses and the aides?"

"They have all left long ago; help here, I'm afraid, isn't very permanent."

"Do you suppose I could have their names and Social Security numbers?"

It may have been gradual and I hadn't noticed, but I realized then that Mrs. Kappleman had become someone else. The voice was higher, the accent gone, the features sharper, the lips thin. There was no more friendliness.

"That's a funny question for a psychiatrist to ask. Who are you, anyway?"

"I'm what I said; I have a card."

"I'll bet you have plenty of cards." She called on the intercom for someone to come and take the trays, even though I hadn't started the pie.

"Could I see Mr. Peckham's old chart?" I asked.

"You can't see anything; I've work to do now."

Then an orderly came in and she said, "Before you take the trays would you show *Mr.* Boyd out."

14

I'D SPENT most of the day on a long trip and hadn't gotten what I came for, but still my ride into town was a pleasant one. I knew that somewhere (if they were all still alive) was an orderly named Samuel Holden, a practical nurse and three aides who believed as I did in the strangeness of Mr. Peckham. I'd learned quite a bit about him too, and now I thought of a way I could learn more.

I knew the year the accident (why had Mrs. Vukov, when she was giving Mr. Peckham's history to the resident, called it an accident and not a fire?) was supposed to have happened. I'd stop at the library and look in their old newspaper files for an account of that tragedy.

I got off the bus in the center of the city and, in a directory at a phone booth, looked up the address of the library. But when I'd walked to where it was supposed to be it wasn't there.

I traveled two blocks in every direction and finally, back at my starting point, asked a lady passing on the sidewalk where the library was.

She pointed across the street. "It's new, they tore down the old one," she said.

This building was glass and aluminum and I'd been looking for one of granite blocks with huge pillars up the front. It hadn't occurred to me that like pens, libraries could be disposable.

Inside I turned brittle forty-year-old pages for over two hours, and finally there it was. All three papers for September 13 had accounts of the fire that had, on the night before, taken the lives of Mr. and Mrs. Werner Peckham. In two of the newspapers there were pictures.

Because of a late summons to the fire department (when the first alarms were turned in by neighbors the Peckham residence was well in flames) and because of an unaccountable failure in water pressure the house had been completely destroyed.

There was unanimous praise for Adrian Vukov. He had suddenly broken from a ring of spectators and had run toward the house. So determined had he been to save the other members of the family that he had dragged a fireman who'd tried to restrain him almost up the front steps. The place was then, according to one paper, a "seething inferno" and to another, "burning briskly," and a groan rose from the crowd as smoke poured from the door Mr. Vukov opened. He disappeared inside and it was thought the fire had claimed another victim—no one knew then how many people might still be in the house. Moments later a giant figure was seen coming out through the smoke. A cheer went up when the crowd saw it was Mr. Vukov carrying the invalid boy, Ernest Peckham.

Back among the onlookers the hero had collapsed in what one paper said was a stupor and another called a delirious state.

As yet the cause of the fire had not been determined. Mr. Vukov was too ill to interview; the boy, Ernest Peckham, suffered from a nervous condition and could not talk, and the other surviving member of the family, Mrs. Vukov, had been visiting friends in another part of the city. Though the house had been large and the family wealthy, no mention was made of servants.

The stories described the various parks the family had donated to the city and the state, their gifts to conservation organizations, and their activities as naturalists.

In the one picture of Ernest Peckham he looked closer to the age of my patient in the hospital than fifteen. The article said Mr. Vukov carried out the invalid, but here the boy was sitting on the shoulders with his legs astraddle the neck of his brother-in-law. Mr. Vukov had "carried the invalid" as a beast of burden carries a rider.

Welcome to the club, I thought, or perhaps this man who had carefully balanced the boy on his shoulders should be welcoming me. Perhaps he should be our president, for his initiation had been more traumatic than mine or that of any of the rest of us. In the picture Mr. Vukov's face was calm and impassive; he seemed unconcerned that his left coat sleeve was burning.

I left the library and started walking to the bus terminal, but I was bothered by something that had happened and needed explaining. Finally I went back to the information desk in the glass and aluminum building. An elderly lady with tinted glasses that went up at the corners had taken the place of the girl who'd sent me to the newspaper files.

"Was the old library a big stone building with pillars in front?" I asked.

"Yes, there is a picture of it on the main floor."

"When was this one built?"

"Eight years ago."

I knew now what had made me uneasy, for I couldn't have seen that old building. I'd first come here when my residency began not much more than six months ago.

I took the escalator to the main floor and found the picture of the building I had looked for. There was no doubt about it: That ought to have been the library. That I'd seen a photograph of it

45

somewhere, perhaps in the pictorial section of the Sunday paper, and had forgotten the occasion was the only explanation I could think of. On my way to the bus depot I tried but couldn't find any more buildings that had been changed.

It was nine-thirty before I got back to the hospital, but I went up to Mr. Peckham's room anyway. I turned on the light and moved to the foot of the bed so I would be in his line of vision.

"Perhaps you noticed I wasn't in today," I said. "But you tell me nothing at all about yourself, so I have been doing a little checking on my own."

Mr. Peckham blinked.

"Did you send me out there like you used to direct Samuel Holden the orderly?"

He lay there looking at me.

"I saw Mrs. Kappleman and I saw her change. I saw the unicorn; it was right in front of me when I ate my lunch. I suppose you know about that and the bus."

There was no change in him, and I went on.

"That must have been frightening when you were in the burning house with the flames crackling all about you. Why did you wait so long before you sent for someone to bring you out?"

Next I tried a critical approach.

"Why didn't you bring more people in to carry out your parents? You see, I know you could have. Don't their screams haunt you?"

There was a change in him finally, but it had nothing to do with what I'd been saying. With the last blink the eyes had stayed closed. Mr. Peckham was asleep.

I had begun carrying a notebook where I kept data on my subject. In it I had the date, time, and content of each message, when I'd checked the EBI and for how long, a description of what had occurred in the day room, notes from my visit with Mrs. Kappleman, and what I'd read in the papers. I entered in it the time he'd gone to sleep and then watched for a while to see if his eyes would open every thirty-nine seconds, but they didn't.

I left them. It seemed I wouldn't reach him by way of his past.

15

ONCE WHEN MY RESIDENCE had first started, Dr. Hahn had given what he called a "know your buddy" party and had hired a limousine that had taken all of us who didn't have cars out to his home (he lived twenty miles outside the city in a big house that stretched along the lake shore) and back to the hospital afterward.

When I asked around I couldn't find any of my buddies who planned on going to the slide show. They all seemed surprised that anyone would want to. I knew if I went out there all by myself in a cab I'd probably get some fatherly advice from Dr. Hahn about how M.D.s should avoid conspicuous consumption. His lectures bothered me more because he kept on talking after everybody understood the point he was trying to make, and it would be even worse with Mrs. Waggoner listening in.

I thought perhaps I should go into Dr. Hahn's office and tell him how I would sure hate to miss seeing the slides he'd brought back but it looked like I wasn't going to be able to scrape up a ride anywhere and that maybe I could ride home with him when he left the hospital. I'd even bring a sandwich so that I wouldn't have to intrude on the family at dinner. After the show I could hitch a ride home with Dr. Shields and his young lady.

I didn't do it because I was perfectly aware, believe it or not, that Dr. Hahn would think I was a nut. I'm mentioning this not to get credit for not doing it, because I'd get more credit if I hadn't even thought of it; but it does show I'm not trying to hold anything back.

Finally I talked one of my buddies into driving me in for fifteen dollars.

47

When we got there a maid let us in and Dr. Hahn took us to the living room, where there were drinks. The house had modern furniture with pictures on the wall that looked like something but not the sort of thing you can quite place, like the colored parts of the Rorschach test.

The fellow I'd come with, Dr. Miller, said, "Say, this might not be so bad."

There wasn't anyone else there yet except older people, who were friends of Dr. Hahn. We had a drink and there was still no sign of Dr. Shields and Mrs. Waggoner.

He drove a low, foreign, racing-type car, not at all the sort I would prefer to have Mrs. Waggoner riding around in.

* * *

With the right kind of accident her face would be badly cut, or rather horribly mutilated, and I'd be the only one who would remember the beautiful person who was hiding inside. I'd give up psychiatry and become a plastic surgeon and, after the three years while I was taking my training and she was hiding in the dark room with no mirrors and no visitors but me, I'd take her in and operate on her. Then the agonizing decision: Should I replace her beauty, as I could easily, or should I just pretend to try to help so I could have her back again all to myself in the darkened room? Pride in my skill rather than my professional ethics finally tipped the balance. What I did was fix her up and tell her it was a failure. Then I put the bandages back on and took her back to the room. A week later or so I came as I had every day, but this time the lights were on. She had seen herself in the window or the toilet bowl or something and she said, "Oh, my darling, don't you know it doesn't matter. You are the only one."

* * *

"Why are you so interested in the Far East, anyway?" It was Dr. Miller back in Dr. Hahn's living room.

I said that I had thought about going into practice over there because it was so crowded everyone was going crazy and where we had one psychiatrist for about every six thousand people here, over

48

there there weren't anywhere near that many and a person could make a fortune. That made more sense to him than if I'd told him why I'd really wanted to come.

Then a couple of residents came who had brought girls with them, and we talked about some of the patients in the hospital. Now and then the girls would say something or ask a question, and I didn't have any trouble talking to them.

When Dr. Shields and Grace Waggoner came in I thought how great they looked together. People like that seemed as though they ought to always be in a TV commercial, walking on the beach holding hands with that music, or she running through the wheat field and he getting ready to catch her. I'd been talking some before that, but when she got there I couldn't say anything. She looked like she did on the ward except she had more makeup and you could see more of her because her dress was shorter and cut lower, too.

Dr. Shields said, "Well, I'm glad to see that there is so much interest in foreign affairs."

Dr. Miller said, "Steve, here, is thinking about going into practice there."

"You can't speak the language, can you?" Mrs. Waggoner asked.

Dr. Shields said, "A good psychiatrist doesn't have to talk much. He can just learn Japanese for 'umhum.' "

They all laughed and Dr. Miller said, "Say, what *are* you going to do about the language?"

"I don't know," I said. "That's the one thing I'll have to work out," and then because that had sounded foolish, I said, "I'm pretty good at picking up languages."

One of the girls said, "Your secretary could be an interpreter while you learned."

Then one of the residents said, "I think he has the right idea. Japan is supposed to be the coming country. They are going to be the wealthiest country in the world, soon."

Dr. Shields said, "Stevie's going to be first in the blain dlain to Japan."

Everybody laughed again. I was watching Mrs. Waggoner laugh, and she looked at me and stopped. I looked away as I'd done often enough before. I wondered if on the way home she would say, "That little Dr. Boyd just gives me the creeps. I'll be glad if he does go to Japan."

He'd say, "Is he a cleepy clumb?" and she'd laugh and snuggle up to him.

A friend of Dr. Hahn joined us then. He was a tall, plethoric, moderately obese man who wore glasses. He told us that he had been watching us and it made him feel good to see such clean-cut young Americans and that sometimes when he saw dirty long-haired hippie kids he wanted to get out of his car and kick them. They were all hooked on drugs and dosed with V.D. and living in communes. He had heard that the birth rate was low in communes because people on drugs forgot about sex, but he thought it was because gonorrhea was making them all sterile and that this was all for the best genetically because it would eliminate degenerates and people who had communist tendencies from the population.

"Louisa Mae Alcott once lived in a commune," I said.

"Now that I don't believe," he said. "You'd have to give me an authority for that statement."

I heard him describe after a pause a beautifully simple plan he believed would save the country. The Public Health Service should start charging to treat gonorrhea. The degenerates, the misfits, the promiscuous of all races would not be able to afford or would not bother with treatment. It wasn't Dr. Spock with his book and a permissive generation who was to blame for our troubles but Fleming with his penicillin and a generation that shouldn't even have existed but should have stayed in somebody's pus tubes.

But more real to me than the red-faced doctor and his message of salvation was Miss Pond, whom he had somehow conjured up with his demand for an authority. She was too thin to be pretty. Her sharp hip bones showed under her brown skirt, but now I knew these were not hip bones but the anterior superior iliac spines that jutted forward so that across her front here she was concave. She had her arms folded under what I guessed, after all these years, were prosthesis and as she told us, her ninth-grade English class, about the Alcott family, tiny parentheses of saliva edged the corners of her mouth. Gentle Miss Pond, once the object of my psy-cholagny (sexual enjoyment from imaginary acts), was now the harbinger of my hypermnesia (an abnormal ability to remember).

The lights started going out then, for Dr. Hahn was ready for his slide show. The first slide was humorous. Photographs of the faces of Dr. Hahn and his wife were set into a cartoon of two people in an airplane headed toward a map of the Far East. They must have been surprised to find big apartment houses and hotels over there, for that is what the pictures mostly were of.

He had a picture of Chinese junks in Hong Kong Harbor and he said, "People are born, live, and die right on these junks." There were pictures of boats that took them across harbors, and the other side of the harbor when they got there. There was a picture inside a temple and he said, "No one can take a picture in here, but I smuggled my camera in under my coat." He may have smuggled his camera in under his coat, but some of the slides looked like he had bought them in a drugstore. The last slide was some flowers upside down and then out, and then upside down again, and then finally right side up.

Then we had coffee and some dessert, cake or ice cream, or both.

Dr. Shields told Dr. Hahn how beautiful it all was and asked some questions. I was afraid he might mention about me going to Japan, but he didn't.

Then Dr. Hahn said, "Dr. Boyd, they tell me that if you don't stop ordering so much lab work we are going to have to hire an extra lab technician."

I supposed they had complained in the lab. There ordinarily isn't much lab work done in a mental hospital.

I said, "Yes, sir." Then I said, "I'll not be ordering so much now," and I wasn't going to. It all came out the same anyhow, and I'd run out of tests to do.

Dr. Hahn said, "I believe that generally it's wiser to sharpen your clinical skills with keen observation and thorough physical examination rather than to rely on the lab to solve all your prob-lems."

I said, "Yes, sir," again and looked at Mrs. Waggoner, but she didn't seem to be paying any attention.

But of course Dr. Hahn wasn't through. "Perhaps even more important than a thorough physical examination is a detailed history. I have often said, listen to the patient long enough and eventually he will tell you what is the matter with him. We should never forget that each patient is a whole person and not a conglomerate of laboratory tests. We shouldn't forget either the therapeutic value of a physical examination. Patients are not fooled; they know that the person who cares about them will spend some time with them. Remember that the first rule of patient care is caring about the patient."

We went home then. I felt like telling Dr. Shields to drive carefully but I didn't, and not because I was thinking of taking up plastic surgery, either.

The morning after the slide show I was leaving Mr. Peckham's room (I'd begun coming over to the ward on days I didn't have to so I'd be on hand for any communication) when Mrs. Waggoner came from another room carrying a tray of medicines. What, I wondered, has happened to you since I saw you last? Where have you been? What liberties did you allow? Or, and this was a more tormenting thought, perhaps it was what liberties did *he* allow?

She closed the door and saw me and suddenly we were walking down the hall together.

"Hello," she said. "Are you on call this weekend?"

"No, there was something I had to check on here," I said.

"Are you really going to Japan?"

There were several answers I thought of that evening like, "Yes, why don't you come along to work in my office?" or "Let's you and I go to Africa and do a Dr. Schweitzer instead." What I said was:

"No, I sort of got trapped into that. I'm not all that good at languages, either."

"Did your prize patient say anything today?" There were little ringlets of hair in front of her ears I would have liked to touch.

"He doesn't really say anything—" For some perverse reason I'd almost blurted out the whole story. "Just words and numbers, not anything like a conversation, I mean. There was 'Hercules thirty-four' and 'Stern'—let's see, 'Stern forty-two' and 'Eagle thirty-six,' as if he were sending me stock quotations—I mean, as if he had been reading about the stock market. I'm not so sure now though."

I was talking too much and rather than stay and give myself away I turned, and still talking over my shoulder, "It's his private language, if I knew enough about him—" I left her.

The elevator was empty and I began lecturing myself: "What a well-formed, small-caliber stool you are, you stupid, stupid fecaliths-for-brains bastard. She asks three questions and you make like you're in analysis. Can't you even be a successful nut?"

The elevator door opened at the first floor and I hadn't stopped my lecture in time so that the people there waited for someone to follow me off. I didn't begin with it again until I was alone in my room.

16

THE DAY AFTER I'd been to Harbor Hospital, I called the stock broker and asked about Unicorn stock and another young man told me there wasn't such a company that he knew of. He said what I must have seen was the abbreviation for United Corporation. They had a preferred issue at forty-two that had been at thirty-nine a few days ago.

I didn't know then what the message had meant. Perhaps it had referred to my trip to the sanitarium *and* the stock, which seemed as likely as either one separately. There was no doubt about the meaning of the words that came next.

I'd been having the usual one-sided conversation with Mr. Peckham.

"Well, I'm ready for the next words, sir. I suppose you know very well I haven't acted on any of your tips. Perhaps you don't know that I'm not going to, either. I can't accept favors when I have no idea what sort of bargain I'm making. I'll say this: If you are grateful because I didn't send you to the nursing home and you are trying to stay here by bribing me, you'd be a lot better off to open up a little and tell me about yourself. That's about the only way you could insure—"

The words "Swan twenty" interrupted me. It was just as well, for what I'd been saying turned out to have been pretty silly anyway.

From the first, the messages had not been frightening or unpleasant, and lately their effect was just the opposite. They had the quality of filling me as well as the room, and afterward they left a feeling of euphoria as though my perceptions were clearer, and if I tried I might be able to run faster or jump higher. I'd begun to look forward to them.

I left the room, took two steps down the hall, and stopped, for Mrs. Waggoner was coming toward me. She was wearing the diamond-patterned panty hose on her long, beautiful legs, and this and her gliding walk and white uniform made me wonder why I'd not made the comparison with a swan before.

You win, I thought, you win, Mr. Peckham. I'll keep you as long as you want to stay, or do anything else you ask of me.

She stopped close enough so I could have reached out and touched her.

"I've been looking for you," she said.

I backed away until I bumped into the wall.

"I know," I said. "I know."

"How did you know? You have a new patient."

"I do?" I said. "I would have guessed you were twenty-five."

"Well, that is how old I am, if that's what you mean. Are you all right? Do you want Dr. Shields to see your patient?"

I was all right. At least my mouth wasn't so dry and the thudding in my chest was subsiding. I was all right because I could see she was unaware of her new situation. In fact, she didn't seem to have changed at all.

Lots of times, I'd had the experience of wanting something in a catalogue or in a store window, but when I got it, almost as though getting it had ruined it, a bright metal part would turn out to be plastic, or something would be wrong with it. That is what I thought first: What's wrong with her? Maybe there are important simulated parts.

I looked at her closely. If anything, she seemed more beautiful now than ever. No, she is real, I thought, this has happened to me and, though she doesn't know it, all of her—the long curves, the tanned skin, the made-up eyes—the whole person is mine.

An emotion surprised me then. I was frightened, not *of* her, though I still felt that, but *for* her and by the responsibility that went with total possession of such a creature.

How would he deliver her? Would she turn up at my room, knocking on the door, and when I opened it would she walk in with her limbs jerking like a puppet's and a blank look on her face like the look on the face of Mr. Vukov in the picture? Would she be a live and passive mannequin for me to play with until I tired of her? That wasn't what I called possession; I hoped I could make Mr. Peckham understand that.

"Do you want to see the patient? I can get Dr. Shields," she said again.

"I'll see him," I said. "You are certainly all efficiency this morning."

She said, "He is in the ward but I don't know if we can keep him there." She started down the hall a step ahead of me. I could have reached out and put my hand where her hip curved and it would be all right. That idea started my heart pounding again, and as though she heard it she looked around and slowed until she walked beside me.

The patient was a lean, wiry, middle-aged man in a bright sport shirt and a pair of slacks with a perfect crease. He was very calm and composed, too much for a man entering a strange hospital.

"I'm Dr. Boyd," I said. "I'm going to be your doctor while you're here."

He said, "I don't really need a doctor but if I have to have one I'm sure you'll do just fine."

"Why were you brought here?" I asked.

"I don't know. There is nothing wrong with me."

Mrs. Waggoner said, "Tell the doctor about the language."

Mr. Sedges, for that was his name, said, "I can speak a secret language no one else knows."

"How did you learn it?" I asked.

"It came to me on the street one day."

"A whole language all at once?"

"Yes, all of it. Suddenly I could speak a whole new language."

"Who do you talk to? Can anyone else understand it?"

"No people you know."

"Who can, then?" I asked.

"Other people, the ones who are coming in the saucers."

"Can I hear it?"

"You won't understand a word."

Mr. Sedges, without warning or change in expression, burst into a series of loud barks and growls that sounded like a large dog at the end of a leash trying to get loose to attack.

When the noise started, Mrs. Waggoner stepped back, and for eleven seconds the pasterolateral aspect of her calf was against my leg. I held her arm halfway between the shoulder and the elbow. Her skin felt cool, and in the three centimeters between the ends of my fingers and my thumb it bulged out a little. When she turned and looked at me I saw the flecks in her brown irises and the lines she had painted along her lids.

A cramp had started in my right quadriceps from holding so still before Mr. Sedges stopped and Mrs. Waggoner stepped away.

She said, under her breath, "That's terrible."

"I thought it was wonderful," I said.

"Thank you, Doctor," Mr. Sedges said. He was a spare, neat little man again.

56

Mrs. Waggoner left us and I examined my patient. I had to repeat several questions because my mind wasn't on my work.

Was I already getting help? Had Mr. Sedges been given his language just to startle my nurse? What was I supposed to do next?

If I followed a purely scientific approach I should not intrude personal desires or emotions into an experiment. In other words, if I investigated the phenomena of Mr. Peckham objectively, as it should be done, if my results were to mean anything, I would play the role of a detached observer and let Mr. Peckham deliver Mrs. Waggoner to me as best he could without any help and, if I really wanted significant results, perhaps some hindrance from me. Then I thought he may have made Mrs. Waggoner available to me but if I don't put forth some effort to accept my prize, wouldn't it be just like my not buying the stocks he had recommended?

Undoubtedly the ideal way of testing what Mr. Peckham could arrange would be to accept but do it in a boorish manner; for instance, step in front of her as she came by with that walk of hers and say, "Congratulations, you have just been awarded as a prize" or "When you get off work today, come up to my room, baby. I'll show you my pens, I'll show you some lifetimes and the time of your life." Then laugh loudly and maybe pinch her if she was still within reach.

As a test that last was the best way, I knew, but I knew, too, that I couldn't do it. When I'd held her arm, it had been involuntary; if I'd planned it I couldn't have done it. If I stepped in front of her to invite her to my room my voice would quaver or get high and she might not even understand me. And if she did and said, "I'll come, what's your room number?"—all that cool skin under the uniform, the curves, the creases, the appendages, it was overwhelming. I had gotten so used to my fantasy Mrs. Waggoner that the real person whose arm I'd held I could probably accept in stages, but I wasn't sure how I'd manage with all of her all at once.

17

IN THE NEXT few days, Mrs. Waggoner's new circumstances seemed to have more effect on me than on her. I watched her more and didn't turn away as quickly when she caught me staring. Once I surprised myself, I suppose more than her, when I winked at her. I hurried off then and avoided her altogether the rest of that day.

The logical step was to ask her someplace, and I'd decided on a movie first and a tavern later after she knew me better. This time I had another reason besides privacy for asking for the date when we were in Mr. Peckham's room; I wanted him to know that Mrs. Waggoner was acceptable to me. On the day I'd planned for it, she was called away again and I went in to see him alone.

"I don't want you to think," I said, "that just because it's almost time for more words from you and I haven't done anything about the nurse that I'm not interested and want to be President or something instead. It's that I'm not used to this situation. Today though, one way or another, I'm going to invite her out. I want to make sure you know about it in case that makes a difference." More than ever I wished that there would be a sign from him that he'd heard.

When I came back to the floor after lunch Dr. Shields and Mrs. Waggoner were at the nurses' station and deep in one of their conversations. What in the world, I wondered, could they be talking about all the time? How was I going to think of enough things to say when I took over?

Maybe somebody pumps him up with a lever, I thought, the

windbag. But I knew he wasn't. He was good-looking, bright, confident, and personable, and he would be a very successful psychiatrist.

As I was passing them Dr. Shields said, "Stevie, won't you come through with another tip?" Then he said to Mrs. Waggoner "Do you know, this guy told me to buy Eagle Industries stock at thirty-six and I did and then sold it at forty-three and now it's forty-six?"

"Eagle at thirty-six," Mrs. Waggoner looked surprised. "Did you invest money in that?"

"I not only invested money, I made money and now this guy," and Dr. Shields nodded at me, "says he's getting more tips from the same place and he won't pass them on."

Mrs. Waggoner was watching me and I winked at her. She may have thought I had a tic, but all she said was, "Maybe it's just as well."

Dr. Shields said, "I hope you haven't quit giving advice about patients, too, because I've got one to ask you about. This is a man who came in this morning. He thinks he has been given the choice of any girl friend he wants, and he picked Mamie Van Doren—"

"Who gave him his choice?" I asked.

"I don't know. Is that important?"

"No, I guess not." I watched Dr. Shields closely, and he seemed only to be giving another case history, as he had at other times when he had asked for my help.

"He picked Mamie Van Doren and now he's mad at me because he thinks she's been trying to call and get in to see him and I've given orders to stop it."

"Maybe you ought to let her in," Mrs. Waggoner said.

They laughed and so I laughed.

"Is he an actor?" I asked. "Can I see his chart?"

"Oh sure, if you think that will help."

Then there really was such a patient.

"He is an accountant," Dr. Shields continued.

"Why is he here? Was he having trouble at work?"

"Only in the last few days. He spent all his time trying to call

59

her long distance and when she wouldn't answer his calls he thought the Mafia was interfering and was holding her prisoner. Now I'm part of the Mafia."

I couldn't imagine myself having such ideas.

Dr. Shields said to Mrs. Waggoner, "You could put on a blond wig and tell him it's all over between you."

She laughed and stuck out her chest. "I'll put on a blond wig and take a look at him and decide for myself what to tell him."

I was watching her and forgot to laugh altogether.

"Does he hear voices?" I asked.

"Yes, he hears the Mafia saying nasty things about Miss Van Doren."

"Try him on trifluoperazine, five milligrams three times a day."

Should I take the medicine myself? If I did and the messages stopped I'd miss them, or rather the feeling that came with them. Perhaps I should give the medicine to Mr. Peckham. Would it be as effective on the sender as on the recipient?

"Well, it's been interesting," Mrs. Waggoner said, "but I have work to do."

Dr. Shields said to her, "I'll be by tonight at seven-thirty."

My confidence in Mr. Peckham was shaken, for that had sounded like a routine arrangement.

Dr. Shields thanked me and left, too, and I stood at the nurses' station wondering what I ought to do.

My investigation of Mr. Peckham wouldn't be complete unless I took the medicine; in fact, I'd have to take it, and if the words stopped I should go off it to see if they would begin again. But I'd do all that later. Surely I'd have enough insight not to harass Mrs. Waggoner, as the accountant had the movie star. The things I'd thought about saying to her, or doing to her, for that matter, were not much different from what I'd thought about when I'd first seen her. But were my inhibitions as firmly entrenched as ever? If she turned me down when I asked her out, would I accept that or would I explain it away and begin acting like the accountant had?

I wouldn't take the medicine, but there was something else I could do.

"You must have a puzzling case." It was Mrs. Bailey.

"Could you hear me thinking?" I asked.

She laughed, "I thought I heard a strange noise." The past few days she had been more friendly.

Before I left the floor, I stopped into Mr. Peckham's room again.

"Well I didn't ask for the date after all; I might have, but Dr. Shields was hanging around all the time. What's more, he's seeing her tonight. That's the girl you promised me, you know. If you can do so much I'd think you could manage it sooner rather than later. One more thing; I think the next step in my investigation will be to see what happens if I try to send you to a nursing home again. This time I'll find out what happens when you actually get there."

I went out the door and started down the hall and then I went back.

"As a matter of fact," I said, "I'm going out now and make the arrangements. You'll be leaving tomorrow forenoon."

I went back to the nurses' station and once again wrote the orders for Mr. Peckham's transfer. The ambulance was to come at 11:00 A.M. the next day.

18

I HAD BEEN in my room eighty-one minutes when I got a telephone call from Dr. Shields.

"Hello, this is Bill."

"Who?" I asked.

He said, "You know Bill—Dr. Shields. Are you doing anything this evening?"

"No, not much," I said. I had been studying some reprints of the British Society for Psychical Research that I'd gotten in the mail that day. It was part of my search of the literature for cases similar to Mr. Peckham.

"I've just gotten a telephone call," he said. "My father has had a heart attack and I'm going to have to leave tonight."

Then he told me he had a date with Mrs. Waggoner for that evening. They had planned to go to a party and just now when he had called her and told her the bad news she had suggested that if he could do it tactfully perhaps he could get Dr. Boyd to take her to the party, as it was one she was almost committed to go to but one she didn't want to go to without an escort. He said, too, that he would loan me his car and that I might just as well use it until he got back and that right now he didn't know how long that would be.

My heart felt as though it were collecting all the blood in my body for each beat.

"Stevie, are you still there?"

"Yes. Where does your father live?"

"New York."

"As far away as that? Why, that's three thousand miles."

"I'm flying, of course."

"I'm sorry it happened—I really am." And I was, because who could qualify more as an innocent victim than this man, clear back in New York, who had never heard of me or Mr. Peckham and maybe not even of Mrs. Waggoner and who now was suddenly terribly sick with a weight on his chest and all because I'd been impatient about delivery schedules.

"It's not the first attack, but this time the doctor says I should come, and I suppose that has to be considered a bad sign."

"Well, better him than you, I guess."

He said, "What? Well, thanks."

"I don't drive."

"You don't drive!" he said like everyone does. "Well, take a cab; I'll pay you back."

"That's all right," I said. "You don't need to."

After he gave me the address of Mrs. Waggoner he said, "And it's Apartment 20."

We hung up and immediately I tried to call him back to ask what they talked about all the time, but there was no answer.

I'll admit I didn't think any more that whole evening about Dr. Shields' father. This is it, I told myself, signed, sealed, and delivered. If I was so sure now of Mr. Peckham you'd think I'd be confident and calm, but I wasn't.

I got in the shower and then got out to call and make certain a cab would come for me. Back in the shower I began worrying about clothes. One of the dozen different Mrs. Waggoners I'd consorted with at night had been a part-time model and very particular about clothes.

I had a suit that was like new that I'd worn on special occasions, like my mother's funeral. It was six years old and had been expensive, but I guessed it was out of style. My other suit was four years old, had cost less and had been worn enough so that the cuffs were frayed. I finally settled on the second one. A shabby suit would be right for a dedicated scientist who had no thought for appearance, but a new suit out of style was not right for anyone.

When I'd finished my shower, trimmed my cuffs, and dressed it was still an hour and a half till the cab was due. I would have had plenty of time to eat dinner but I didn't, and that was a mistake.

I tried self-hypnosis for a while. You know, how you lie down and relax one group of muscles after another till you are completely relaxed; but I got afraid maybe this time for the first time it would work, and I'd wake up at 2:00 A.M. and wonder what I'd forgotten to do.

I called and got the correct time and set my watch, called, and made sure the cab would come and then went downstairs and bought a package of cigarettes in case she smoked, and all the time I was wondering what I was going to say to her.

In my imaginings there had been no long discussions while we learned about each other. I was able to guess her convictions and make terse comments such as: "Most men are chauvinistic pigs," or "Less than 10 percent of the world's population are using 50 percent of the world's resources to cause over 90 percent of the world's pollution," or simply "Power to the people." She moved closer then, her eyes widening in incredulous recognition of an ally, and our understanding was so complete long conversation was unnecessary. Now faced with a whole evening in the company of a real Mrs. Waggoner, I wished I'd rehearsed something other than slogans.

I'd allowed myself enough time so that the driver of the cab dropped me off at the address a half hour early. It was a square three-floor building that looked like all the others on both sides of the street, but inside in the hall I saw that this one was where she lived. There was a directory—white plastic letters pushed onto ridges of black felt—and opposite Apartment 20 was "Mr. and Mrs. Waggoner."

Every day she stands here, I thought, and bends down a little to look in her mailbox. She climbed those stairs a few hours ago; her legs went out of sight right there, and now she's up there somewhere getting ready for me.

Her arms overhead she shrugs from side to side and a pastel-flowered dress slides down and hesitates until the movement that began in her shoulders reaches her hips, or she's bathing, the breasts glistening, the nipples just hidden by the soapy water, or she's spraying with one of those sprays they advertise.

I went outside and circled the block until it was time to go up to her.

19

HER APARTMENT was at the front of the building. I rang the bell and heard steps inside. The door opened. It was Mrs. Waggoner.

"Come in," she said. "I'll only be a minute."

She was wearing the pastel-flowered dress I'd seen a few minutes before and then I remembered she had worn it at the slide show. Her hair was pulled back and she had on low-heel shoes.

I walked in and said, "You have a nice apartment." It was what I'd planned to say if she asked me in.

She looked around as if she were seeing it for the first time.

"Oh, it's all right; I don't like apartments very well."

She offered me a chair and sat on a couch on the other side of a coffee table. She'd been wrapping a package, and now she went back to this, folding the striped paper at the ends and fastening it with transparent tape.

"It's nice of you to do this," she said. "To come with me, I mean."

"Oh, I wasn't doing anything anyway." Immediately I thought of better answers.

"Would you hold your finger there?" She had ribbon around the package and was tying the knot.

I stepped to the coffee table and suddenly we were in the same position as when I'd talked to the governor. Now, though, instead of a uniform she was wearing a dress cut so low I was confronted with much of the superior and more of the medial aspects of her breasts.

The knot was pulled tight over my finger and I heard a whispered "Shit" as the ribbon broke.

"You can take your finger away for a minute."

I stood in front of her as she unrolled more ribbon and wound it around the package.

"Yes, you certainly have a nice apartment," I said.

"Lend me your finger again."

This time the ribbon held and the knot was tied.

"It's a present," she said, "a perpetual calendar for the people where we are going."

She stood up and crossed the room and turned on the television.

"I always put this on when I leave so it will seem someone is home."

I committed two breaches of etiquette then. I let her reach the door first and open it and she had to hand me the package to hold while she locked the door. I should have taken the package before

65

we left the apartment, but I was preoccupied with a comment about television, a comment that was ready when we were out in the hall and it was too late to use it.

On the stairs, I provided us with something to talk about. I stumbled and while my feet bumped along the edges of the steps I began juggling the package in front of me. Finally I took off in a magnificent leap, sailed down the last third of the stairs and out into the hallway and didn't catch my balance until I'd run up against the outside door.

I turned back to Mrs. Waggoner, who had been watching from the stairway.

"It certainly is a nice apartment house," I said.

"Are you all right?"

"Oh, yes, I'm fine."

She came down the stairs and on her way picked up the card that belonged with the present.

"Are you sure you're all right?"

"Oh yes, I keep in good physical condition," and I did feel steadier now than I had all evening.

I opened the door and held it open with one foot while I tried to straighten the bow on the package, but it kept falling off to one side.

Mrs. Waggoner barely glanced at her present as she went by.

"Don't worry about it. They will never notice," she said.

We had started down the sidewalk when it occurred to me that she might think I was driving.

"I don't drive," I said.

"I know, we'll take my car."

Does a person open a car door for a woman who's going to drive? I didn't know and didn't even know which car was hers.

She said, "Here it is," and stepped off the curb.

I sprinted around behind the car and managed to get to the door ahead of her. I tugged at the handle but it wouldn't open.

"It's locked," she said.

She unlocked it and before I could intervene had opened the door herself. I did close it for her and went around to my side and got in.

It's odd, I thought, how jumping down the stairs or running to get the car door open settled me down. My body was ready for strenuous exertion, and when it was used that way I felt better.

Could my physiological turmoil, the dry mouth, the jerky limbs and thudding pulse all be simply caused by fear, a psychosexual adolescent's fear of heterosexual contact? Perhaps there was another mechanism at work.

After all, not long ago in man's evolution the approach to a mature female must have meant combat with other males, and I remembered a television show where a female mountain goat had patiently watched two males rear and butt each other again and again. Natural selection favored the stronger in these contests, of course, but wouldn't there be an advantage too for the male who automatically responded to the presence of a receptive female with an intense physiological mobilization for an emergency?

To investigate the hypothesis one would have to monitor blood pressures, pulse rates, respiratory rates, blood sugar and adrenalin levels and even blood pH in animals and humans during their preparations for mating. In man comparison could be made with boxers who were preparing for a bout. The levels in women would have significance too, for there would be no reason for such a reaction in the female.

"Why didn't you learn to drive?"

"We didn't have a car."

When I was reminded where I was and who was driving my symptoms of sympathetic nervous system stimulation recurred which, unless I subconsciously suspected that Mr. Waggoner had hidden in the back seat and was ready to attack me, was a count against my theory.

"I'd think a doctor would almost have to have a car."

"That is true and I am definitely going to learn to buy a car," I said.

She told me about the party we were going to. It was a housewarming for friends of hers who had just moved into their first house.

"I went to school with Sue Hinney," she said. "That is their name, Walter and Sue Hinney. I suppose I had better warn you this won't be the same sort of crowd as was at Dr. Hahn's. These people are on the whole more liberal. I suppose you'd even call some of them revolutionaries."

This was a cue from my fantasies, and I gave the answer I'd often given before.

"Revolution is as American as apple pie."

I was ready for the reverse upright handshake. It would be a spontaneous gesture of recognition of our mutual sympathies and our first physical contact in a sequence that would eventually have her hiding me in her apartment from the FBI.

"Walter Hinney is an attorney and has to deal with all sorts of people."

Before I dropped my hand and turned back in my seat I'd caught a glimpse of the long curve of her calf, the pallor over the pattelae, and the tapered thighs that got so close together at the edge of the flowered dress.

"They bought a sixty-five-year-old house that I think is about the nicest house I've ever been in. It was in terrible shape but they are fixing it up. I helped with some of the painting myself."

She was occupied with a left turn before she went on. "I think I like old houses more because we lived in a modern house and every few years it was all redecorated and remodeled so that nothing had a chance to get old."

"What kind of house did you live in?" she asked.

I'd been listening to her voice as much as what she said, and it was a moment before I realized she had asked a question.

"We lived in trailer courts mostly," I said.

"You lived in trailer courts and didn't own a car?"

"We did have a car. My father had a car but he was killed in an accident when I was eight and after that my mother and I kept the trailer but we didn't have a car."

She turned a corner and said, "We are almost there now."

We were on a street of big old houses of various architectural styles of which pillared southern mansions and English country homes predominated, but there were Spanish haciendas, Italian villas, and a fanciful production that was probably Byzantine. They were set well apart on wide lots in the shelter of towering trees, and almost without exception they showed evidence of neglect and disrepair.

"Until Sue and Walter bought their house, I didn't even know this neighborhood was here," she said.

But I did, I thought.

An impression had been growing in me that I had once known this street very well and that I was barely kept from remembering the details of that time by a subtle distortion of everything around me.

"I think that is my favorite." Mrs. Waggoner pointed to a massive house of light brick, with various roof levels, several wide chimneys, and a carriage drive.

Still plagued by the feeling of *déjà vu*, I asked, "Is it possible that there is a trailer court nearby?"

"No, there isn't."

I tried to imagine the lawns mowed, the houses with fresh paint, and the windows without the "Rooms for Rent" signs and found that I couldn't. The shabbiness belonged; but something else was wrong. It was as though we had stumbled onto a movie set where everything had been designed and was maintained to show a decayed opulence.

Could that be the answer? Had a picture been filmed here that I had seen on television? It didn't seem possible that I would know what the houses were going to look like before we came to them.

"There it is." She was pointing ahead.

20

AFTER MRS. WAGGONER parked the car, we walked the last half block. My feeling of being on the verge of remembering when I'd been there before was stronger than ever.

"Don't you think it's just beautiful?" she asked.

"Yes," I said. But not quite the same as it once was, I thought. If I knew what was changed I'd know from when I remembered it.

It was a half-timbered house with rhododendrons growing under low casement windows. The lawn was dry and sparse from the shade of huge trees, but it was one of the few I'd seen here that had been mowed.

I followed her up a curving brick walk, across the porch, and through the open door. In the big entrance hall, the feeling of familiarity was gone.

On the left a broad staircase went up, and across from this, set in an almost room-sized alcove and flanked by high-backed benches, was a huge rough-brick fireplace. Lights with shades like gold lily blossoms were set in bronze sconces on the dark paneled walls.

A tall man with moderate temporal baldness and horn-rimmed glasses left a group of people and came over to us. He was Walter Hinney.

After Mrs. Waggoner had introduced me, she said, "And here is something for the house, but it's not very grand for a place like this."

He said, "You know, it's not how much it cost that matters, it's how much we can get for it when we are selling everything to keep up the payments."

Mrs. Waggoner laughed and said, "Now I wish I'd bought you something else I saw, a genuine Spode plaque of President Harding."

A pretty, blue-eyed woman with a round face and dark hair came up to me with her hand out.

"Hello," she said. "I'm Sue Hinney."

Mrs. Waggoner said, "Sue, this is Dr. Boyd."

"Are you a psychiatrist?" she asked.

"I'm a psychiatric resident," I said and unnecessarily added "too." There was no need to call attention to my being a substitute.

"Well, I may need you before this night's finished," she said. "And I need you right now," she said to Mrs. Waggoner.

Mrs. Waggoner went off with her to help in the kitchen, an arrangement that evidently had been planned all along. Mr.

Hinney got me a drink, introduced me to a social worker and his wife, and then left to meet other guests.

They asked me what sort of doctor I was, what was my specialty, and how active I'd been in the free clinics that had been started in the city. I told them I was an M.D. and a psychiatric resident and that no free clinics were convenient to the hospital where I was in training. I didn't add that the idea of working at one of the clinics had never occurred to me.

The social worker, who was no bigger than I but had a full beard and fierce eye said, "I don't suppose that patients find their illness very convenient either."

When I agreed, he said, "I think the finest chapter in the history of American medicine is being written by the young doctors at these clinics."

He and his wife saw someone else they recognized and left me.

I got myself another drink from a bar that had been set up in the corner of the dining room and began a tour of the house. Mrs. Waggoner was right: It was grand.

Except for the living room, where a design of foliage and flowers was molded in the plaster, all the ceilings had dark wood beams; there were four fireplaces; each room was paneled in a different kind of wood; and the floors were intricate parquetry. It looked bigger because the Hinneys were short of furniture; in the library with its marble fireplace and bookcases with leaded glass doors there were only two chairs and a table, all of wicker. One room must have been meant for plants: It had a tiled floor with a drain in the center, and two of the walls were mostly windows.

When I went back to the dining room to get my glass refilled, it was crowded (altogether seventy-eight people came to that party) and warmer (later even with the doors and windows open the temperature reached 28.89 degrees Centigrade) and more noisy.

I edged my way between clusters of people and backed up once to give the right-of-way to a man carrying two drinks. As he passed me, I noticed, from the level the ice floated, that the solution in the glasses had a specific gravity of 0.97.

When my glass had been refilled, I worked my way out of the

congestion about the bar and into the center of the room. Here I sipped my drink and listened to the half-dozen conversations that went on around me. That I was following them all simultaneously didn't seem extraordinary to me.

Finally I interrupted a girl who had been explaining a problem and how she hoped to solve it to a group on my left. She had thought she was pregnant, and when her doctor told her this wasn't so had decided her morning nausea was due to seasickness from the motion of her water bed. Unwilling to give up the pleasures the bed offered otherwise, she had been adding gelatin to the water, hoping that the mixture would be solid when she slept but would liquefy when she had intercourse.

"Your approach is ingenious," I said, "but doomed to failure. The amount of heat required to liquefy five hundred gallons of gelatin is more than would be generated by the most abandoned group orgy.

"You are trying to form a thixotropic gel, and to accomplish this you should use ferric oxide, or better yet, bentonite."

The young lady said, "I'm trying to form a tricksy what?"

"A thixotropic gel. However, a word of caution. Bentonite is hydrophilic, so don't add too much or the bed may swell and burst with considerable force."

"Thanks a lot," she said. "I can get my kicks without going to bed with a bomb," but I had turned to another group.

"Actually the first historically recorded death from air pollution was that of Pliny the Elder in A.D. 79, and as has been generally true of cases in recent times, he was rendered more susceptible by being afflicted with chronic bronchitis."

"Was he allergic," a man asked, "to the farting of the chariot horses?"

Before the laughter had subsided and I could explain how that ancient encyclopedist had died, an erroneous statement in another conversation caused me to intervene there.

"It is not true that there are no endangered species among insects. You have not considered the plight of *Pulex irritans*, the human flea: Unless prompt action is taken, future generations will know this heritage from Neanderthal man only by studying dried specimens in museums."

I turned completely around. "The panes in the windows here are small because when the houses were built that this is copied from people couldn't make bigger pieces of glass."

There was one last question: A man asked, "Where did he come from?"

I explained I was a psychiatric resident from the state hospital and then, since the talk around me had subsided and my glass was empty, I left them and started working my way back to the bar.

Moments later in the living room I found Mrs. Hinney and a circle of friends admiring an antique corner chair she had bought at an auction. She said that yesterday after waxing and polishing it in preparation for the party she had noticed sawdust and small white worms on the carpet. She had thought when she bought the chair that the worm holes might be fake; now she wished they were.

"Were they alive?" a woman asked.

"Yes. See for yourself."

Mrs. Hinney tilted the chair and tapped it and her friends stooped to examine the floor beside the chair.

"Those are worms, and they are alive, but what looks like sawdust must be worm shit," someone said. There was an argument then over what the fine white particles on the floor should be called—sawdust, worm droppings, worm sign, or perhaps disinterred worm turds.

"I believe," I announced, "that the worms are the larval stage of the deathwatch beetle. There is an ancient superstition concerning this insect. It is believed that it makes a clicking noise when someone in the house is going to die. Actually the sound is the adult beetle knocking its head against the wood, which is its way of sounding a mating call. Now if everyone will be quiet for a moment, let us see if we can demonstrate this interesting phenomenon."

I got on my knees and held my ear to the chair. I couldn't hear a thing. "Sometimes they will answer a watch," I said and held my wrist watch against the chair. By now, the crowd around me

73

was so noisy I couldn't have heard the beetles if they had all been trying to answer me at once.

Somebody asked what I was doing and someone said, "He's listening to the Beatles on the smallest record player in the world."

Someone else said, "He's a psychiatrist," and there were other comments like, "He says there are some long-haired worms screwing in the furniture." "They have a word for what he's doing but I can't remember it." "How about you showing us the mating call over here against the wall, Doc," and "Maybe they will do it if you drop dead."

I felt a hand on my arm then and Mrs. Waggoner pulled me up.

"I don't know what's going on," she said, "but I don't think any of you are a bit funny." She led me away.

"I want to apologize for those people," she said. "I guess I should have known better than to leave you alone."

I said, "I don't think you should, either."

"There is going to be some food in a few minutes."

"Did you have an orthodontist?" I asked.

"How many drinks is that for you?"

"This is about my fourth, but you shouldn't get the wrong impression. I didn't fall; I was trying to demonstrate an interesting phenomenon, but it's too noisy here. You don't suppose I could come back tomorrow and listen to her chair, do you?"

"Oh, she wouldn't mind if you still want to."

"Did you have an orthodontist?" I asked.

"Yes."

"He sure did a great job."

"Wait right here," Mrs. Waggoner said, and she had me sit on the bench by the fireplace in the hall. "Now stay there and I'll get us something to eat."

She left and shortly afterward two couples came over to me.

One of the men said, "Are you Dr. Waggoner, the psychiatrist?"

"No, I'm Dr. Boyd, a cicesbeo."

"What you said isn't true, is it? Fleas are not threatened with extinction."

"Human fleas are," I said.

One of the women said, "There ought to be a society to protect them." She was upset.

"Think of it this way," I said, "and perhaps it will be easier for you. Only a fraction of a percent of all the species that have been evolved are alive today. It is as natural for species to die as individuals—maybe more so. When man became hairless, fleas never adapted to the change and kept their characteristics that enabled them to crawl through fur. Man obliged them for thousands of years by wearing animal skins, but they failed to take advantage of a second chance. When the furs were discarded and man chose a more sanitary life it was a question of time, but *Pulex irritans* was doomed. I'm not saying we shouldn't try to preserve the species, but surely the fleas are as much to blame as man for the trouble they're in."

The taller of the two men had very distinct freckles that were visible even in the dimly lit hall, and now he turned away and walked across to the other bench.

"It's a put-on," he said. "He's made it all up."

"Oh, no, didn't you ever wonder why there are no more flea circuses?"

"What's that got to do with it?" he asked.

"*Pulex irritans* was the only flea with the strength and stamina to perform, and so with his passing so also passes the flea circus."

He considered my answer carefully, then took two quick steps toward me and threw his drink in my face.

Somewhere behind me a woman began repeating, "Get Walter, get Walter Hinney."

The man asked me to go with him outside. I started to explain that I was supposed to stay right there but he paid no attention to me. When it seemed I'd have no choice but to disobey Mrs. Waggoner because he'd lifted me up by the front of my coat, he shoved me solidly back on the bench.

Mr. Hinney got between us then and soon the man, still arguing and his freckles brighter than ever, was being urged and pushed on his way out of the hall by a circle of friends.

"Now what's happened?" Mrs. Waggoner was back with a plate of food.

75

"It was just an insecure person's reaction to what he presumed was an ego-threatening situation."

"I could see he was mad, what happened?"

She wiped my face and clothes with a napkin while I explained in more detail.

"And that's true about the fleas."

"Yes."

"It's just silly enough to fight about I suppose."

"What pen are you carrying tonight?" She felt for it through my coat and then reached in my shirt pocket and pulled it out.

It was a Parker Duofold, blunt-ended, bright orange, and very big. She held it in both hands and turned it slowly back and forth.

"It's just beautiful," she said, "and so huge."

"Yes," I said, and began at once to explain about it. "It was called a Duofold Senior, and it dates from the early twenties. It was—"

"What's this? Someone must have been studying hard. Look how they have bitten it." She held it up and I saw on the cap small indentations made by a student years ago in an examination. Then smiling and looking directly at me, she put the pen between her teeth and gently bit the end.

"Take that coat off," she said suddenly. "You look too warm."

After she had folded the coat on the bench beside her, I asked, "In psychiatric nurses' training—" I had to push the words up through a narrowed glottis, "In your nurses' training, do you study Havelock Ellis?"

"No, but it's a groovy name," she was smiling again, "and anyway I'll bet I know what he says."

"I don't think I'm a bit hungry," I said.

"Eat something," she said. "We have all kinds of time."

I found that I was hungrier than I'd thought, and the food was very good.

She sat beside me on the bench and now and then made a comment like "That dressing is homemade, not bought" and "That's fresh crab, not frozen."

"Why aren't you eating?" I asked.

"I had some in the kitchen." Later she asked, "Why did that man call you a chiropractor?"

"He was angry."

Before I'd finished, Mr. Hinney came back and apologized and offered to have my suit cleaned.

"That's all right," I said. "You don't need to."

Mrs. Waggoner said, "I kind of like it. They ought to make Scotch after-shave lotion," and she pulled my head over and nuzzled my cheek.

"How do you spell 'Hinney'?" I asked.

"It's spelled with an 'e,' " He spelled his name.

"Without the 'e' it's the opposite of a mule."

"I know," he said.

"A mule is the product of a male donkey and a female horse—"

"Yes, I know," Mr. Hinney said.

"And a hinny is the opposite. But you probably get tired of hearing that."

"No," he said, "actually you'd be surprised at how infrequently people mention it."

Mr. Hinney left us and I said to Mrs. Waggoner, "I guess you'd say I just pulled a *Varanus exanthematicus*."

"A what?"

"A *Varanus exanthematicus* when I mentioned that about Mr. Hinney's name."

"What's that?"

"Oh, it's an African lizard that's supposed to put its foot in its mouth when it's agitated."

"No," she said, "I wasn't going to say that."

When I'd finished, Mrs. Waggoner first offered to take my plate and then took my arm. "Maybe you should come along. You can see where we painted."

As I was following her to the kitchen, we passed the social worker and his wife.

"You know, Babylonians gave them up," I said.

He looked at me blankly.

"The free clinics, the free clinics, the ancient Babylonians gave them up."

But Mrs. Waggoner was tugging on my arm. "Come on, let's not threaten any more egos tonight."

She showed me the big kitchen and told me she and Sue Hinney had painted it.

"That's two coats and five days' work," Mrs. Waggoner said. "Three days just on the windows."

"Did you ever see a bigger kitchen?" she asked.

I said that I hadn't and she said, "No, I don't suppose you ever have."

We found the Hinneys then and said goodnight. Outside in the dark the feeling of knowing the neighborhood was gone altogether.

21

I DIDN'T MAKE the mistake of trying to open the locked car door, and I did close it for her. On my way around to my side of the car I was surprised that I had not noticed before how much the taillight resembled an orthopteran ovipositor.

After we had traveled two blocks I said, "You certainly have nice friends."

"Where did you learn that about their name? I've known him five years and I didn't know that."

And immediately superimposed on the dashboard was a textbook open to page 187, where in the second paragraph the mule and the hinny were compared. I could have read it if I'd wished, but that was unnecessary: I knew what was on both the pages that faced me. Then I mentally turned a page and I knew everything there too.

"I majored in animal husbandry for a while in college," I said.

"What is animal husbandry?"

"It's learning how to raise and take care of animals."

"I like animals," she said. "I always brought home animals that were sick and tried to take care of them. I don't know how my parents put up with it."

"Were you going to be a veterinarian before you decided to be a doctor?" she asked.

"No," I said. "I was going to be a rancher. I think I was influenced by the early Marlboro ads."

She was wise enough to know I wasn't joking and kind enough not to laugh at me anyway.

"When did you decide you wanted to be a doctor?"

"In college; I majored in several different things and finally went into medicine because it took so long to finish and I liked school."

There was an interval before she asked,

"Why did you go into psychiatry?"

"I thought perhaps I'd find out what was wrong with a person who liked school better than anything else."

The answer to the next question, what had I found out, would be embarrassing, for none of it had been complimentary, but she didn't ask it.

"I think that's why a lot of people go into it," she said.

"How about you?" I asked.

"I wanted to find out what was the matter with everybody else," she said. "That's what I used to tell people, anyway.

"How could you afford to go to school as long as you wanted to, or rather, as long as you did?" she asked.

"My father was a steelworker and he was killed in an accident on his job. My mother was paid a monthly settlement for that as long as she lived, and she worked as a nurse too." Which didn't exactly answer her question but was the way it had been.

"What were you doing by that chair?"

I explained about the larvae on the floor and how I had listened for the adult beetles.

79

"And that's all true, like the fleas?"

"Yes."

"And what you said about the lizard?"

"Yes."

She parked the car.

"There won't be a place any closer," she said, "but tonight at least I've got someone with me."

While we were walking to her apartment house I thought, how much more protection Dr. Shields must have been, a head taller and fifty pounds heavier.

At her door I hesitated and she said, "Oh come in, I won't really bite."

What, I wondered, had she meant by that?

"Anyway," she said, "you have to call a cab."

When we were inside she said, "Now sit down and I'll get us a drink."

She stepped into the kitchenette and a moment later came out again.

"And if you want to use the bathroom it's right in there," and she pointed to a short hall.

I sat on the davenport and watched a movie, and before I'd decided which war it was about she was back.

"I'd have asked what you wanted, but vodka is all I have."

She turned off the television and sat beside me on the davenport. She was more than close, she was against me.

"Now," she said, "what I want to know is where you learned all this odd information and how do you remember it all?"

Where had I read it all? A kaleidoscopic jumble of pages from encyclopedias, books, magazines, journals, and newspapers appeared before me, and no part of one obscured another, so that I saw and knew the whole of every one. Not only that, the places where I'd been when I'd come upon each item, the classrooms, libraries, our trailer, a bus station, the different waiting rooms all were as real as Mrs. Waggoner's apartment, and all seemed to surround me simultaneously. And the scenes that were called up brought with them the feelings I'd had then, the excitement at going off to school, the apprehension of waiting for a dentist, the despair and hopelessness I'd felt in the waiting room of the hospital when I knew my mother was dying. It was too much.

"I'm sick," I said, and ran for the bathroom.

Here with my knees planted wide apart I watched dressing, homemade not bought, and crab, neither fresh nor frozen, reappear in swirling chymous gushes.

During an interval in the unproductive retching that followed I heard Mrs. Waggoner beside me.

"How do you feel now?"

She was sitting on the edge of the tub with a washrag in her hand.

"Like a planarian."

"Whatever they are they must be miserable."

"It's a small flatworm whose digestive tract ends with its stomach so that it regurgitates what it eats."

"I never thought I'd know that, and I certainly wouldn't have guessed I'd learn it here," she said.

Another attempt at complete eversion was so violent it caused the short audible passage of flatus.

"I guess we can scratch the planarian bit," she said.

I looked up at her and immediately she slipped off the edge of the tub and kneeled on the floor beside me. "I'm sorry," she said, "I'm not a bit funny," and she began to wipe off my face with the cold washcloth.

There were more spasms of lessening intensity and at increasing intervals.

Once I turned to her and said, "This is very humiliating."

"Then I won't tell anyone about it if you don't."

Later she said, "I ate exactly what you did, but not so much, and I feel all right."

When I was sitting on the edge of the tub and blowing into toilet paper the last pieces of potato salad out from under my turbinate bones I tried to arrive at a diagnosis.

Mrs. Waggoner, who now was alternately wiping up my trail and flushing soggy Kleenex down the toilet, did not seem to be affected. The symptoms had occurred too soon after ingestion for it to have been food poisoning. Was it a case of ordinary alcoholic gastritis? I'd had four strong drinks, and on an empty stomach that would probably be sufficient. It was more than I usually drank, and why, for that matter, had I drunk so much?

The usual warning signs of intoxication, the slurred speech and lightheadedness, had been absent. Actually, the only evidence of being drunk I'd had was the impaired judgment that had caused me to be the butt of some jokes and that had made someone angry enough to throw a drink in my face. Instead there were the seemingly limitless stores of information on obscure topics and the ability to recall my sources in minute detail; both were an exaggeration of what had happened to me at Dr. Hahn's slide show.

Now Mrs. Waggoner brought me a toothbrush and a pair of pajamas.

"You can't go home tonight. I'll make up a bed on the couch."

I didn't argue but brushed my teeth with what I hoped was her toothbrush and put on what I was sure were Mr. Waggoner's pajamas. A few moments later, carrying my clothes in one hand and holding up the pajamas with the other, I came out of the bathroom to find Mrs. Waggoner sitting on the edge of the couch that now had sheets spread on it and a pillow at one end.

She got up. "I'll leave the light on in the hall and in the bathroom just in case you wake up and feel sick." She went into her bedroom and closed the door. I stretched out on the blankets. Was this her pillow? I couldn't be sure.

What had happened to me that evening? Subjects under the effects of hypnosis or certain drugs were often able to recall memories that were not available to them otherwise. In the sessions of that sort of thing I'd seen when there had been any results at all, the examiner had had to suggest most of the answers. This had been something else entirely.

I tested then how far back I could go with the vivid recollections, and above me my mother and father began lurching backward about the trailer at a sickening speed. With them the nausea came again. I was relieved to find that I could wipe out the wild scene as easily as I had called it up.

And Mrs. Waggoner, I'd certainly muffed it there. How much allowance could Mr. Peckham make for such bumbling?

The bedroom door opened and Mrs. Waggoner, the woman I'd seen so often in the nurse's uniform and lately in the pastel-flowered dress, was outlined by the light in the hall. She was encased in a flimsy fluted tube that extended from her shoulders and breasts to the level of the perineum.

"And if you wake up and feel really well," she said, "I'm in here." She went back into the bedroom and left the door open.

22

I WAS BACK at the hospital but all the patients were gone, except Mr. Peckham, who was in a bed in the center of the men's ward. He had a cluster of people about him, each busy with some chore. A barber was cutting his hair; a physiotherapist was giving him passive exercise; an aide was feeding him; another aide was giving him a manicure; an orderly held a urinal; and a nurse was waiting with a tray of medications.

The men were in white hospital uniforms but the women were dressed like Oriental dancing girls with long skirts and bare waists. At the end of the room the rest of the staff were arranged in tiers, as though posing for a photograph.

Mrs. Waggoner in her short nightgown and I in a white uniform with brass buttons and gold epaulets stood to one side and watched as one by one Mr. Peckham's attendants finished their duties and left to take up a place in the pattern of spectators.

As I moved forward, the last of the group, a flustered physiotherapist, tucked the sheets about Mr. Peckham and followed the others. Mrs. Waggoner took her place beside me, and now that all was ready handed me a blood pressure cuff. I took from my pocket a gold-embossed stethoscope set with cut jewels and placed it around my neck.

When I turned back the sheets the reason for the physiotherapist's distress was obvious. Mr. Peckham had six arms.

His body was segmented and the skin, except where it was thickened at the joining of the parts, was translucent, so that I could see a sluggish pulsation in the branching blood vessels and indistinct outlines of internal organs.

I replaced the sheet and glanced at Mrs. Waggoner. Had she seen? Her downcast eyes and impassive face gave me no clue. This time I carefully exposed only the right middle arm. It had a cold and waxy feel, and no matter how gently I handled it my fingers left indentations.

I saw now that what Mrs. Waggoner had handed me was not a blood pressure cuff but a cylindrical can. A fine purplish dust adhered to the perforated top.

There was a whispered, "Quick, use it."

I turned and the mascaraed eyes in the pale face were wide and pleading. "Only you can do it. Please use it now."

There were other dreams. Mrs. Waggoner tried to pull me from a sea of printed pages that I was slipping deeper into while a colossal Mr. Peckham, so huge his head and shoulders occupied the whole horizon, watched something in the distance behind us. The material engulfing me was continually added to from above; I could see it first as tiny silver flakes that glinted in the sky. It was Mr. Peckham's dandruff.

Then my mother was trying to pull me out. She was far too weak for such exertion, and I said, "Don't, Mother, you'll bleed again."

This she promptly did and the emaciated legs became two spirally turned crimson pillars. The soaked pages gave me some purchase, and I was able to climb out.

I was standing by the davenport and ran to the bathroom and retched again. Then I came back and fell into a sound sleep.

23

I woke in daylight. My watch had stopped, for in spite of my freakish memory I'd forgotten to wind it. But had that even been memory?

I could recall one by one the scenes that had crowded the room the night before and could see again my sources for the odd information. But I couldn't add more. In the text of animal husbandry I knew and saw clearly the four pages I'd seen already, but when I tried I couldn't look farther.

As I dressed in the bathroom, spots on my rumpled clothes reminded me of my violent and embarrassing illness. And after all of that she had said, "If you feel really well—"

How did I feel now? Hungry, for one thing, but no headache. If I hadn't made such a fool of myself I'd have to say I felt great. I looked in the mirror and tried to wipe smeared material from my coat. I needed a shave, my clothes were sour-smelling, but I felt great.

When I went back in the living room Mrs. Waggoner was up. She sat with her chin on her hand, on the edge of the couch watching me. She was wearing an old blue bathrobe and gold slippers with turned-up toes.

"How is Mr. Encyclopedia this morning?"

Her eyes were puffy from sleep, her makeup was smudged, and her hair tousled. I thought this is Mrs. Waggoner in the world she comes to when she leaves the hospital, and I've followed her here.

"I feel fine," I said.

"Great, call the hospital and tell them you're sick."

"What?"

"Tell them you're really sick, 'cause I have three days off. Tell them you will be back Tuesday. Now get out of those clothes, and at ten o'clock I'll take them out and get them cleaned. They will be ready by five."

When she stood up the robe fell open. She started to slip the coat from my shoulders.

"And if we can't find time at ten o'clock I'll do it on Monday," she said.

Suddenly we were kissing. I was able easily to palpate her ribs and vertebral spines and was surprised that the fullness of her breasts had concealed such an asthenic body. She pulled away.

"Agh! Take off that coat."

I slipped it back on.

"Dr. Shields won't be there. No one will be there. I have to go to the hospital."

"No, you don't; no one's indispensable. That vegetable will be there when you get back."

When I stepped around her and started for the door she said, "All right, Dr. Kildare, take off your coat. I'll make you some breakfast and drive you in."

I turned back to her, and because of all that had gone on before but more especially because of Mr. Peckham's promise, I pushed aside the robe to fondle her breast through the night-gown. She backed away from me and wrapped the robe around her.

"Keep your hands to yourself. I'll get you a razor, and don't ask whose it is because I don't remember."

After I'd shaved I went into the kitchen and sat in the alcove. She'd poached me an egg and made some toast.

"I'll come in this evening," I said.

"What makes you so sure you'll be welcome here?"

What would she say, I wondered, if I told her?

Then she sat down with a cup of coffee. "Did you ever get sick like that before?"

"No, never, not like that."

"How much did you drink, anyway?" she asked.

86

"Four drinks. But I hadn't eaten, I was too excited."

"You aren't very excited this morning."

"Yes, I am." I reached across to touch her face like I had when I'd talked to the governor.

"Oh, stop it," she said. "If you're not going to stay, eat your breakfast."

When I'd finished and we were ready to leave she said, "You can carry that coat."

I slipped it off again and folded it so only the lining showed.

"I'll pick you up at four o'clock," she said.

"With Dr. Shields gone I won't be able to get away so soon. You had better make it five-thirty."

There was a pause before she answered.

"All right then, five-thirty."

Before I went to my room and changed to my uniform I stopped at the floor and canceled the arrangements I'd made for Mr. Peckham's transfer. Later that morning when I pulled back the covers and saw the little man without any sections and only two scrawny arms, I'll admit I felt relieved. But he wasn't a deteriorated schizophrenic either, for one coincidence can follow another, but eventually things can't be explained so simply.

The transformation in Mrs. Waggoner (a few minutes ago I'd caught myself looking for her on the ward and then remembered the girl with the flushed skin and mussed hair whose voice had gotten huskier as she planned our weekend) had been—there was no other word for it—miraculous. But a supernatural explanation was what I had to guard against, for when I accepted that as the answer then by the usual standards I'd no longer be sane. I hadn't made much progress in accounting for things otherwise, and each new demonstration made my task more difficult, but explaining it was not so important to me as that I kept on trying.

As I had expected, there was another message for me that day.

If you were walking down the street with a friend and someone you passed said, "Fox sixty-eight," no matter how clearly, you would probably turn to your friend and say, "He said something that sounded like 'Fox sixty-eight.'"

That wasn't the way it was with Mr. Peckham. His words were

clearer than speech could be, and if I left the room not knowing what they had meant I didn't worry about it, or about anything else, for that matter.

I didn't see all of Dr. Shields' patients, but I saw all who needed seeing, and in spite of the extra load I finished early. I called Mrs. Waggoner and told her I'd be through at four o'clock after all and then went over to my room and took a shower. The suit that had been more or less responsible for my even getting there that morning I rolled up and threw away.

When we lived in the trailer and I used to stay all night sometimes with a grade school friend of mine, Boney Stivers, there were always plenty of paper bags around, but now the only one I could find was so small my pajamas stuck out the top.

I stopped by the ward (there is a rule here that if you're going to be gone overnight you are supposed to leave a phone number even if you aren't on call) and gave the afternoon nurse the number where I could be reached.

She looked at the paper bag and asked, "Isn't that Mrs. Waggoner's phone number?"

I said, "I don't know, is it?" It was an impertinent remark I probably wouldn't have made if I hadn't heard from Mr. Peckham that morning.

Then I went downstairs and waited for Mrs. Waggoner.

24

ON THE WAY into the city she stopped at a grocery to shop for our dinner. At the check stand, I was going to pay but, though there wasn't much in the cart, I didn't have enough money.

She said, "I've got some good steaks and a bottle of wine. That's why it's so much. You can buy next time."

When we got out of the car to go up to the apartment I carried the groceries and she took my paper bag.

"Is there a note here on how to fix your cereal?" she asked.

I'd started to tell her before I realized it was a joke and we both laughed, but even so I was a lot more at ease walking upstairs beside her than I'd been the night before when I'd come up to take her to the party.

I left our groceries in the kitchen and asked if I could help. She told me to put something on the phonograph. When the first record started she said,

"I'm glad you like that, for I think it's my favorite piece."

"What is it?" I asked.

"You didn't play that on purpose?"

"I just picked some out of the stack. I don't know much about music," I said.

She went back to measuring vodka into our glasses.

"I do like that very much, though," I said.

It was a person playing a piano but not what I'd call a catchy tune.

She handed me my drink. "How would you like your steak?"

"Well-done," I said.

"That's what I thought it might be. If you're tired, you can stretch out on the couch."

"No, I'll stay here," and I sat at the table in the alcove in the kitchen.

"What sort of day was it with Bill gone?" Bill? I thought, and then remembered Dr. Shields.

"I was surprised," I said, "everything went very well. I missed you, though," which was true, for now and then I had found myself looking for her.

"Well, it's your fault if you missed me. I was ready to screw all day except for maybe a half hour now and then for a nap or something to eat."

When I didn't answer, she said, "Do you want to take your bag and go home?"

"No," I answered. I was wondering what would have happened if I had stayed with her and let Mr. Peckham go to a nursing home. I might still be watching her cook our dinner but I wouldn't be as relaxed and confident, that was certain.

"And you get one drink," she said, "and the wine when you eat, and that's all." I didn't ask for more; I was uneasy about drinking anything.

As I sat watching her, the music changed. Now there were themes and counterthemes that sometimes surprised me but more often I anticipated and waited for. I began to make variations in my mind, and Mrs. Waggoner's movements about the kitchen became a dance with a piano accompaniment. Once I touched her where briefly under the loose-fitting dress y^2 had exactly equaled $2px$. She turned and looked down at me.

"These are just about the most expensive steaks I ever bought. It would be a shame not to finish cooking them."

"I'm afraid," I said, "that the afternoon nurse recognized your phone number."

"That's all right, I don't care," she said. "I guess I'm beyond shame."

I laughed and she didn't, and I wasn't so sure it had been a joke.

"It is a very unusual number," I said.

"Why? It's just a phone number, isn't it?"

"No, if you use digits instead of the prefix the lowest factor is 191." The trouble had started again.

That was the first indication that a facility with numbers was part of the symptoms, and then at once I knew what had been meant by "Fox sixty-eight." Mr. Vukov would be sixty-eight now; he was the fox. Not only was I certain Mr. Peckham wanted me to check on his brother-in-law, it was clear to me how to do it.

After that I only pretended to sip from my drink. But I knew there was no way I could avoid sharing the expensive wine.

When we sat down to our dinner, she asked,

"Did you ever say Grace in your family?"

"No, but it is a beautiful name." It was an automatic reply from my fantasies.

From then on, the answers didn't come so easily. The trouble was that what I would ordinarily have remembered was buried in too much vivid detail from too many incidents. For instance, I could have said my father cheated at cards without describing a particular game of hearts and enumerating what was held in each hand and the play of each trick, and I could have said my mother smoked too much without making a comparison of the cigarette butts in the ashtrays as to numbers and mean length of those with and those without lipstick.

I finally got started on a safe subject and one I really enjoyed talking about. I told her how pens were given as graduation presents and after that were considered a part of a person and weren't loaned to write a line for someone else. They had been used for intimate confessions in diaries and for love letters, wedding invitations, signing a mortgage, and then the monthly payments. Finally when the checks each month were too many and there was no place to sign for more money, some of the pens wrote suicide notes. They had recorded everything that person had done, and now with the person gone and most likely all the paper he had written on gone, too, all that was left was the fountain pen, which seemed sad until you thought of how it was now with ball-points, for now there was nothing left.

She took away the plates then and brought back a frozen dessert that she must have made during the afternoon.

She said that if she walked any special way it wasn't because of ballet lessons, for she hadn't had any. I told her about watching her on the ward and asked if she knew she had made a conquest.

"Of course," she said. "How could I help but know? Sometimes I think if I went and visited the Pope he'd renounce celibacy. I'm just that way and partly it's my own fault, but I don't remember anyone who ever looked more thoroughly stricken than you."

I remembered to ask the most important question of all as far as my investigation was concerned and because I'd been rehearsing it all day and wondering about the answer, it came out stilted sounding.

"And could you tell me, my dear, at what precise time you decided you would grant me your favors?"

"Precision is the one thing we can do without," she said, "and right now is when I'm going to grant my favors and grant and grant and grant."

When she got up from the table, so did I.

"You go in the bedroom," she said. "I'll be in in a minute. If you had let me know sooner what you planned for me, I could have started on my pills, but for now I'll have to use that damn diaphragm." And that was as close as I ever got to an answer to my question.

Her bedroom was cluttered. The bed was unmade and there were clothes draped over a chair. I took off my coat and picked my way through the shoes on the floor to hang it in the closet. I'd turned around and slipped off my tie when she came in the room. As though she were all alone there she unzipped her dress, let it fall to the floor, and then kicked it aside. A moment later, she had completely undressed, and only then did she look at me. As I'd done on the ward when she'd caught me staring I turned away and was about to hang my tie in the closet when she took it from me and tossed it aside.

"We'll get you some clothes," she said, "that will be worth taking care of."

Then in a scene more erotic than I had imagined I alternately joined Mrs. Waggoner in fumbling at my buttons or traced with both hands the outlines of her body. I forgot and she didn't know or, more likely, we both forgot that the shoes would have to come off before the pants, and when we knelt to undo the laces we bumped heads. She sat on the floor then beside me while I finished the job alone.

At last when she was on the bed beneath me and I was assuming what manuals call the preferred position, I was rendered helpless by a prolonged orgasm.

"When this occurs among primitive nemerteans," I spoke from four inches of her left ear, "the sperm burrow through the female's skin."

25

AFTER WHAT Mrs. Waggoner called her behavioral therapy (she told me where to get a towel and then propped herself on her elbows and supervised while I wiped her off), she grasped me and began an explanation of a way to determine who would be up first in a baseball game by taking alternate hand-holds of the bat and then interrupted herself and said, "Never mind, I win," and got astride me.

Then I gave what I thought was a superlative performance. The next morning, though, I had to revise my standards for, gauging by the reaction of Mrs. Waggoner, I did even better.

In one aspect of sex, I had more experience than she: I knew that an ejaculate that is smeared from the umbilicus to the pubes and runs off onto the bed does not represent a dangerous loss of protein. But when she fixed me three eggs and six sausages for breakfast and told me not to bother with the directions for making my cereal because I wasn't going to get any, I didn't argue.

By noon it was too warm to stay in her apartment, so we packed a lunch for a picnic in the park. When Mrs. Waggoner suggested getting beer, I said I'd rather have pop, and that is what we bought.

I wondered how much I should tell her of my unique sensitivity. The night before there had been two ounces of vodka in my drink and I'd taken less than a fourth of that or less than 7.5 cc's of alcohol when the symptoms began. This morning when Mrs. Waggoner had wakened me with her system to see "who would be up first" there had been no trace of it, though again I'd remembered everything that had come to me under its effects.

When we drove in the entrance, Mrs. Waggoner noticed the name on the bronze plaque.

"Christ—if I'd known what they called this place, I'd have gone somewhere else."

"He's not so bad," I said. "He's no trouble. I mean, he's not demanding."

"I know," she said, "and I don't know why I feel this way, but he's the first patient I've ever seen who makes me think euthanasia might be a good idea."

"Don't say such things," I said.

"Why not? It's what I think. To me there is something about him that's not even human. I wish you'd transferred him when you were going to."

A moment later, she said, "Why in the world did you ever tell Bill—Dr. Shields—to invest money in something you had heard from him?"

"This looks like a good place," I said.

Later after we'd eaten our lunch, we lay in the shade of a large maple tree.

"What games did you play when you were little?" she asked.

I told her I hadn't been very good at games.

She said, "You should have had some of the lessons I had."

Her father, she thought, had wanted a boy, and when she had come along had decided a girl wouldn't be so bad provided she was a champion. He had started her at ice skating lessons before she was four and then, three years later, when it became obvious she wouldn't get to the Olympics as a skater, he'd gone on to swimming, tennis, skiing, horseback riding, and last of all, golf lessons. Once when she was twelve he'd even timed her to see if she might not be a distance runner but that, thank goodness, had only lasted one day. So she had turned out about average at more sports than anyone, which wasn't good enough for the Olympics except that you might enjoy them more as a spectator.

"Where did you learn about baseball?" I asked.

"That was in girl's gym. It's funny, that was one of the few games I liked."

Once she asked if I'd really gone into medicine just because I'd have to spend a long time in school.

"Yes," I said. "That, and of all the people I met in college the premed students were the most enthusiastic about what they were doing and worked the hardest and sometimes even cheated to get good grades. Their one goal was to get into medical school. I thought if they were all so sure being a doctor was great, I might as well try it, too."

"I'm glad you didn't become a tattooed rancher," she said. "I never liked the way they looked at their cows."

We spent the afternoon there until finally in the evening the mosquitoes drove us away. On the way home, we stopped at a delicatessen and bought sliced meat, salad, and bread for our meal.

When we got up to the apartment I put her record on the phonograph and again the music changed as I listened and Mrs. Waggoner went into her dance.

Once more I involuntarily put my hand on her hip.

"It's not a question of steaks tonight," she said.

Hand in hand then but neither walking nor dancing, we were carried along by the cascading notes into the bedroom.

Later that evening after we had eaten our dinner, I questioned Grace again as to when she had first felt an interest in me.

"There is something I want to talk about," I began.

"I've been wondering when you'd get around to this. Well, let's do the dishes and then we can talk in bed."

"No, this is important. This is something I must know."

"You want to know if I've been screwing Bill. The answer is no. But I don't suppose you'll believe it."

"Who is Bill?"

"Dr. Shields." I was sure she had mimicked my voice.

"Well, that was not what I was going to ask."

"You mean you're not interested?"

"Well, not now, anyway. Now I want to ask you about something else."

95

"O.K. I'm ready. But why can't you ask questions in bed? We can talk one on top of the other as well as across this table."

"No, now, I really need to know this. When did you first decide we could form a liaison?"

"Form a what?"

"Form a liaison—have an affair."

"I like the 'form a liaison.' It has a tony sound. Is that a medical term for a doctor screwing a nurse?"

"Be serious for a minute. You didn't need me to take you to that housewarming. They were all your friends."

" 'Were' my friends is right."

"But you could have gone without an escort."

"Yes, I could have."

"So why did you? When did you decide?"

"What difference does it make? Are you writing a book or making a report? Maybe because of your early training you brought out the animal in me."

I couldn't get a straight answer. She joked at first (once she said why worry about the first time she wanted to lay me when the next time was already here, and once she said she had always been attracted to men who vomited), and finally, when she was getting angry, I gave up.

26

THE NEXT morning, she began fixing me the same breakfast.

"Two eggs would be enough," I said.

"How are you going to make that wallpaper paste on two eggs?" She kept on with her cooking. "And anyway I've decided the only way I'm going to get over you is to get you fat."

"You won't need to come and get me this evening. I'll meet you in town. At the library at six," I said.

"Does this have something to do with Mr. Mushroom?"

"Yes," I said. "I want to look up in old newspapers all I can find about a fire he was in once. It may help me to understand what he is talking about."

"Bring your checkbook with you and tonight we will buy you some clothes," she said.

At twelve-thirty, I looked at my schedule for the rest of the day. Two appointments were down to give individual psychotherapy, and I left notes for the patients canceling these. There was a seminar on interviewing techniques that I skipped altogether. Somewhere in my room there was a folder that told, among other things, what trouble I'd get into if I missed too much of that sort of thing. I decided I'd read it again when I had time, and at twelve-forty I left the hospital.

I wore my white uniform into the city. On the bus I could have been a barber or a waiter, but when I went into the other hospital and put my stethoscope around my neck, I was a doctor again and, I hoped, a doctor everyone would assume was on their staff.

I walked the halls, spoke to anyone I saw who was dressed like myself, and ignored everyone else. It was a bigger place than I'd expected and finally I had to go back to the entrance and, at a window marked "Information," ask for directions to the record room.

When I'd found it, I stopped at the first desk inside the door and interrupted a young black woman's typing. I wanted, I said, to see the record of a Mr. Adrian Vukov, and I handed her a card where I'd written: his name, the date of admission (that was a drawback, asking for a forty-year-old chart was bound to attract attention) and the diagnosis. She took it back to another desk in the big room where she and a gray-haired woman held a conference. Once when they both looked at me, I resisted the impulse to walk out of the room and the hospital and catch a bus back to the apartment where Mrs. Waggoner would be waiting. I told myself that even if I were caught I was not breaking any

97

law I knew of and looked directly back at them while I twirled my stethoscope in front of me. The younger woman left, was gone six minutes, and came back again with only my card.

"Do you want just this admission?" she said.

"No, I'd like to see all of them."

She went out again by a door at the far end of the room and returned almost at once with four boxes of microfilm and a chart.

Did I dare, I wondered, ask where their viewer was?

"Do you know how to work the viewer?" she asked.

"I'm not sure; do they all work alike?"

"I'll show you." And she led me over to their viewer, put in a reel of film, and found a chart for me.

"That was a long time ago. We don't often get asked for charts that old," she said. "Now if you need more help, just ask."

In the next hour and a half I learned a lot about Mr. Vukov and was interrupted just once when the elderly woman stopped as she was passing.

"Are you finding everything you need?"

"Yes, thanks," I said.

The record the young woman had left in the viewer was for a ten-day period Mr. Vukov had spent in a charity ward eight years before the fire. Then he had had an appendectomy. He had given his occupation as student and his mother as his nearest relative and had gone back to live with her again, presumably, on leaving the hospital, for hers was the only address he'd given when he was admitted.

The chart I most wanted to see was on the next roll of film. I twisted a knob and forty-year-old records blurred past on a lighted screen. Sometimes I'd stop to check the number and then I couldn't help but follow a few frames to see whether someone named Nellie Lovejoy had survived, relying only on her body's defense and not penicillin, a temperature of 105 degrees, a wild delirium, and a cough with a tenacious sputum, or I'd read how a resident was justifying a radical new treatment: "the instillation of blood in the veins."

Once where I stopped there was an outline of a man's body and an explanation beside it that the parallel lines marked second-degree and the crosshatches third-degree burns. It was Mr. Vukov. His arms and chest were mostly lines; a patch of squares marked the place on his left arm where I'd seen the coat burning in the photograph. I backtracked until I came to when, a half hour after he'd carried Mr. Peckham out of the house, the doctors here had first seen him.

They had puzzled over why he was stuporous and confused and, looking for fractures, had X-rayed his skull. Then they dressed the burns with Vaseline gauze, started intravenous solutions, ordered sedation, and left their patient in the care of the nurses. That night and during the three-week period of his hospitalization, while the interne, the resident, and later the attending physician were content to describe his level of consciousness, his general condition, and how his burns were healing, the nurses had made voluminous notes. They charted when they had turned him, recorded his intake and output of fluids, included the inevitable description of the bowel movements but, most important to me, they quoted all they could make out of the words he had mumbled and shouted.

Often he had repeated, "No, no, no," until an entry was made, "Sedation given and patient quieter." There were phrases: "You'll give it away," "Don't give way," "I won't," and "It's too hot." Once he had shouted, "It's on my back."

The police came the day after the fire but were told an interview was impossible. On the fourth day the patient was conscious intermittently and the next day the police were back. A nurse was probably unaware of the implications of her observing that "Patient seems nervous after visit with the police." Still they must have been satisfied, for I couldn't find where they had come back to see him again.

There were more visitors. The nurses called some of them friends and some business associates, but they didn't say how they told them apart. His wife was not mentioned; if she had come to see him she had been mistaken for a friend.

He had been moved at the end of the first week because, "Patient wants transfer to a ward. He states he wants people around him." Two days later he was back in a private room. The other patients had been disturbed by his shouting at night.

Twelve years later, Mr. Vukov returned to the hospital for treatment of gastroenteritis contracted in Mexico.

He had been a student when he'd had appendicitis and an attorney at the time of the fire, but now he was simply an "executive." If his wife stayed away before, she visited him daily now, and once at least a nurse thought, "The patient was upset by wife's visit." There had been penalties to pay for his rise in fortune: The student took no medication but the executive took sleeping pills nightly and still suffered from insomnia and nightmares.

Nine years afterward Mr. Vukov, an executive with the odor of alcohol on his breath, had been in an auto accident and had had, as an outpatient, a laceration of the forehead sutured. He was "in the company of a belligerent and obviously intoxicated female companion."

The last chart was three years ago. Mr. Vukov was admitted then for chest pain that had begun on a flight from Japan and was first thought to be a heart attack; X-rays, however, showed a pneumothorax, which cleared in six days, and he was discharged.

For the first time he admitted he'd had a venereal disease; he had contracted gonorrhea sixteen years earlier. Perhaps the "intoxicated female companion" was to blame. The time was right and there were mitigating circumstances: Under the heading "Family History" was "Wife has been a paranoid schizophrenic many years."

He went into more detail when he described his work. He was the executive director of an organization called The Creatures of Earth Alliance.

I returned the microfilm and chart to the young lady who had gotten them for me, thanked her again, and left.

Back on a bus and on the way to the library I wondered again what, if anything, Mr. Peckham wanted from me. There had been no mention that the police had questioned the nurses or looked at the chart. Perhaps terrible crimes had gone unpunished and Mrs. Vukov had lost her sanity from suspecting her husband. Was I supposed to expose the executive as a murderer and arsonist? If I reported all I knew to the police without mentioning the messages, of course, would it do any good? After so many years something called the statute of limitations, I thought, wiped out even the worst crimes. I would have to have a clear directive from Mr. Peckham before I confronted the executive myself. In the meantime, I would find out what I could about The Creatures of Earth Alliance.

In the library, I went back to the files and looked for more articles about the fire, and I found one in a paper I'd looked at before. Three days after the fire and buried in the middle of only one newspaper there had been a reference to it again. The police were examining the possibility of arson and then, perhaps suggestively, it said in the next paragraph that Mr. Vukov, who was still hospitalized and in critical condition, had not been interviewed.

And that was all. I looked carefully in all the newspapers that had appeared for six weeks afterward, but it wasn't mentioned again. Strange, I thought, front-page news one day, one more item a few days later, and then nothing more. Before I left the library I looked for The Creatures of Earth Alliance in the telephone directory. It was listed and I copied down the address. Then I went outside to wait for Mrs. Waggoner.

Twenty minutes later I was still standing there. I'd go to the apartment if she hadn't come in another hour.

* * *

When I rang the bell, a man came to the door. Tall and solid in a light blue sport shirt that was taut across a powerful chest, he was a bruiser.

Mr. Waggoner was back to claim his beautiful wife. I caught a glimpse of her sitting in the wing chair, frightened and subdued, her dark eyes wide, her face a white mask.

"I've come to take Mrs. Waggoner to the hospital: An emergency has arisen and her presence is required there."

Mr. Waggoner folded his arms so that the brachial veins stood out on the huge biceps. The angle of his gaze down at me was at least fifteen degrees.

The only indication of my rising anger was that my voice was a little lower in timbre and I spoke more slowly and distinctly.

"Yes, a patient's life is at stake. He requires her ministrations."

"Sorry, buster, something has come up" (no one with so much tooth decay should smirk like that) "right here at home that is going to require her ministrations, so buzz off."

But I slid by him into the room.

"Get your coat, Grace—pardon me, Mrs. Waggoner—and whatever else you may need, for we are leaving."

"Listen, buster, I hope you know how to turn a corner in flight; otherwise you're going to be in the apartment across the hall." It was a long speech for someone as angry as he now was, the smirk was gone, the slightly pockmarked (no, they were acne scars) face was red.

From the chair in the corner I heard Grace's strained voice.

"Stephen, please go; you don't know what he's capable of."

Then I saw the long purple bruise on her upper arm. "I'm quite sure that I don't," I said, a shade slower and even more distinctly.

I stepped to him then and grabbed the shirt at the first buttoned button, where the coarse hair stands out in a brushy shield. Blows rain on my head and shoulders, but still holding him at arm's length, my hand level with my eyes, I twist the handful of shirt and hair.

Gad, this time how I'd like to go all the way.

The blows are weaker now and I stop the twisting (mother said with my temper I might end up in the pen), but now my fist is supporting the purple face with the distended veins and bulging eyes.

The blows have stopped altogether and still holding him at arm's length (a fall from that height could cause a serious head injury) I lower him to the floor. Now I feel for the flickering pulse.

"He'll come around in a few minutes," my voice is normal again.

Grace clings to me; I can feel her breast against my arm.

"Get your coat. Let's leave before he comes to. There's really no need to put him through this again."

"Stephen, Stephen," she cried.

* * *

In a car at the curb Grace leaned sideways across the seat and held the door open.

Still a little shaken, I got in beside her.

"I'm late and I'm sorry but traffic was terrible and for at least a minute I've been trying to get your attention. Why were you looking so fierce?"

"I was subduing Mr. Waggoner."

"I'll tell you about him someday but for now you can forget him. But why in the world are you wearing that? And the stethoscope," she pointed to my pocket. "It's too late now to give me a physical exam. Whatever I may have you've already caught it."

"I was in a hurry, and I didn't want to go back to my room," which was partly true but still a lie.

We spent the next two hours shopping. Much of what we bought had to be altered but we brought home with us shirts, ties, shoes, socks, and a postcard and stamp. That evening I sent off a note to The Creatures of Earth Alliance asking how I could become a member.

We got up with the alarm the next morning and like thousands of couples in similar apartments, dressed, ate breakfast, and went off to work.

From then on, we were usually able to take our days off together, and sometimes when I was on call Grace would stay overnight in my room. There in the bed where I had lain with my fantasies I would often awaken to the weight of a startlingly real Mrs. Waggoner, sound asleep and in the process of mounting me.

27

FOUR DAYS LATER an answer to my card came in a brown manila envelope with twenty cents in canceled postage on it. There were degrees of membership that cost from ten dollars for an ordinary member who got a publication every two months for a year to one thousand dollars for a lifetime member who had special privileges in the centers the organization mantained around the world.

The Alliance studied the habits of animals to see how species could be maintained. A unique approach they used was to offer participation to wealthy people who could thus harmlessly satisfy their desire to hunt.

There were beautiful full-color photographs of wildlife. Some not so beautiful showed what might be any great white hunters beside their fallen game, but a caption underneath these explained the animals had only been tranquilized and banded and soon would get up and run off to resume their natural state. A few of the pictures gave the impression that among their employees were young women who wore bikinis to study dolphins in Florida.

It was a coincidence I'd come to expect. Earlier that morning I'd gotten another message: Dolphin sixty-seven.

By complicated ways, like adding the amount of postage, the number of pages, and the largest of the pictures, I could arrive at sixty-seven, but later I was handed a piece of paper that had the number indelibly marked in it.

At two twenty-three in the afternoon Mrs. Bailey told me Dr. Hahn wanted to see me in his office.

I'd never been there before. It was bigger than any office

needed to be, and dark, with the light coming from behind him so you couldn't see his face very well. There was a dusty fern in a brass planter by the window. I think it was real.

I looked around for a calendar that might still have the month of June showing with the seventh circled—6/7 or 67—but the only calendar was his desk calendar, and it showed August, as it was supposed to. He thought I was polite and asked me to sit down, but I kept on looking for numbers. I did sit, though, when he asked me again.

He started telling me about a letter he'd gotten, and I knew that was where the number would be.

Mr. Peckham's relatives were complaining about my doing experiments on him just because he was a hopeless case. They had tried everything, all the different kinds of treatment and all the best doctors (they had even taken him to Europe once, which was something I didn't know anything about), and they had resigned themselves to the fact that nothing could be done. Now I was getting everybody stirred up and causing expectations that couldn't be fulfilled and so they wanted him changed to another doctor.

Dr. Hahn stopped, but I didn't say anything. "I took the liberty of looking over his chart. I don't see where you're doing anything," he said.

"I'm not, sir, except that I'm talking to him more than I'm sure anyone else has."

"I don't quite understand," Dr. Hahn said, "how he happens to be here still. Perhaps the thing for us to do if the relatives are dissatisfied is transfer him to a nursing home. It seems to me that's long overdue anyway."

"Oh, no, sir," I said. "He has made tremendous improvement in the few weeks I've had him. He's making a real effort to communicate for the first time in years."

Dr. Hahn looked surprised. "Do you think he is an interesting case?"

"Indeed I do, sir; one of the most interesting in the hospital."

"Well," he said, "we must always remember we are a teaching institution as well as one that provides patient care. If you think we can learn something from him of course we will keep him."

"There were other charges in the letter," Dr. Hahn was embarrassed. "They or rather Mr. Vukov claims this patient hasn't talked in forty years. He says that you're hallucinating, that you admitted it."

"But I don't admit it," I said, "and anyway he wouldn't know if Mr. Peckham is talking or not. He's never been to see him."

Dr. Hahn was writing. "Well now," he said, "just what has he been saying?"

I stood up suddenly and pulled at the front of my trousers as though I were saving the press. He had been doodling; I couldn't make a sixty-seven out of it.

"Words mostly, animals and numbers. Nothing you could make sense out of," I lied. "Fox sixty-eight, Dolphin and, let's see, sixty-seven—yes, that was it: Dolphin sixty-seven or Dolphin *six seven* and Swan twenty and Eagle thirty-six. There have been more but I can't recall them," I lied again. Remembering nonsense would be as abnormal as talking nonsense.

"Did you call his sister?"

"Yes. I talked to her and a nurse on the telephone for six or seven minutes." I wished I could see the letter, then I'd know how much to say. "I was trying to explain the treatment technique of Harry Stack Sullivan, the altering of thought processes from paratactic to syntactic. I think they confused empathy, as he stresses it, with telepathy," I said, "which is understandable."

"Yes, of course," Dr. Hahn said. "Dr. Eng tells me you've made remarkable improvement as far as your clinical work is concerned."

"Thank you, sir."

"There is one thing I wanted to talk to you about. Your attendance at the seminars has fallen off where once it was perfect. Remember, more prizes go to the stayers than go to the spurters. I like to think of the clinical material here as the bricks that you use to build your skill, but the didactic material, that's the mortar; without the didactic material sometime it will all fall down and you and your patient will be trapped in the rubble."

"No, sir." But he hadn't said, "You don't want that, do you?" this time. "I mean, yes, sir," I said.

"I think I'll let you answer this letter, but you might let me see what you write before you send it." He handed it to me in its envelope. "I can see you're enthusiastic, and we need that, of course, but I wouldn't raise their hopes if I were you.

"One other thing, Stephen, we must always remember that the chart is a record of a person, and for some of those here it's the only record of their existence over a fair interval of their lives; as such it deserves as much respect as the patient himself. Don't write anything, I always say, on a chart you wouldn't want to read and explain in a court of law."

He was talking about the note I'd written when I'd heard the first words. I'd always thought his lectures wouldn't bother me if there was no one else to hear them, but I was wrong.

I went back to the ward and dictated an answer to Mr. Vukov's letter. There was no reason to expect improvement, I said, but there was a change in Mr. Peckham, for he was not so much talking as verbalizing. No new or experimental treatment was being used; I had merely tried to show him I was very interested in the content of his communications (I thought about having the typist underline "communications" but decided against it). I would like to meet him and discuss Mr. Peckham's case anytime he could arrange it. In the last sentence I suggested that Mr. Peckham would be disturbed by a change in doctors.

I didn't say anything about hallucinations or another charge that was in the letter. Dr. Hahn hadn't mentioned it, but Mr. Vukov had accused me of turpitude in my conduct with Mrs. Waggoner.

On our way to the parking lot Grace said, "If you're not going to tell me what Dr. Hahn wanted I won't ask, but I won't drive you home either."

"You're going to be mad," I said, and handed her Mr. Vukov's letter.

Partway through I heard, "What's this?" She had come to the paragraph that mentioned her. "I'm not mad so much as scared," she said. "How could this person know about us so soon?"

"I don't know," I said, "unless someone called for me after four o'clock some day and got your number."

"But how would they know it was my number? It's spooky."

We sat in the car while she read it again. "I thought it was always moral turpitude," she said.

"I'm sure that's what he means."

"It's a good grade of paper for a poison-pen letter." She held it up to the light. "See," she said.

In the watermark I read "over 67 percent cotton fiber."

28

WHEN I CALLED the psychiatrist who had been Mr. Peckham's doctor at Harbor Hospital I couldn't get through to him but had to leave my name and number and wait for him to call me back.

His voice was deep and resonant and like his name must have been a great asset.

"Dr. Boyd? Dr. Adler here," he said in the manner of a character in an English movie.

"I'm a resident at the state hospital. There is a patient here who you took care of a number of years ago. A Mr. Peckham."

"Yes, I remember him—a schizophrenic."

"I'd like to arrange to meet you and discuss his case."

"I'm afraid there isn't much to discuss; he was a schizophrenic, completey withdrawn even that long ago. I wouldn't have any more to tell you."

"Well, just recently he's talking."

"He is? Maybe it's another Peckham. My patient was Ernest Peckham, a member of a wealthy family here."

"It's the same man. He was at Harbor Hospital twenty-five years ago."

"And he is talking? What is he saying?"

"Just words and numbers. I thought perhaps if I could go over them with you you could help me work out the meaning."

"Work out the meaning? I'm afraid that's impossible. In the first place, I don't think I could help you. He said nothing at all when he was my patient, and in any case I couldn't find the time. Sorry."

"One more thing," I said quickly, because he'd been about to hang up. "Could I get your permission to see his old charts from Harbor Hospital?"

"Certainly," he said, "you have it, but of course you'll need the written permission of the family too." And this time he did hang up.

His response had been predictable. He was a busy psychiatrist and I must have sounded like an eager resident who intended a miracle cure for a hopelessly chronic case.

Later the same afternoon when I called The Merri Hours nursing home and talked to Mrs. Hatch, the owner, it was obvious that with her Mr. Peckham had made more of an impression.

At first she thought I was going to send her a patient and told me how lucky I was for she had one bed left for a woman, but if I wanted to send in a man she could make a few changes and take him too. She had a lovely place with well-qualified help and a registered nurse on every shift.

"I'm calling about a patient who was there eight years ago," I said, "an Ernest Peckham. Do you remember him?"

There was an interval then of five seconds.

"Who did you say?"

"Ernest Peckham, a little man. He would have been forty-seven years old."

"He can't come back here."

"I only want some information about him."

"He was here so long ago I don't remember him very well."

109

"Why wouldn't you take him back?"

"I won't. He was a disturbing influence. He was noisy."

"How was he noisy? What did he say?"

"That's so long ago I can't remember. Why do *you* want to know, anyway, Doctor?"

"Well, he has started to talk and I wondered what he had said in the past."

"Well, I can't help you. If you ever have other patients, remember us," and she started again explaining what fine care they would receive.

"Is there anyone else there who could tell me more about Mr. Peckham, or do you have his old chart?"

"There isn't anything about what happened on the chart, and no one here could tell you any more than I can."

She told me once more to send anyone else, said goodbye, and hung up.

I decided then I'd go out to Merri Hours. I'd tell Mrs. Hatch that my referring a whole series of patients to her nursing home depended on my finding out what had happened eight years ago that she didn't want to talk about or didn't think anyone would believe.

Grace had such an antipathy for Mr. Peckham I couldn't ask her to spend part of a day off looking with me for the nursing home where he had once been. It was an unpleasant job I'd have to take care of myself when I could find time for it.

On days that Grace came with me into Mr. Peckham's room I'd say things like "Good morning. Are you going to talk today so the nurse can hear you?" though of course I knew he wouldn't.

When I was alone I reported to him about the letter and my telephone calls and how my investigation had temporarily reached a dead end, but there was no more response from him than there had ever been.

One day while I was telling him how much easier it would be for me if he could somehow lessen the feeling of dislike (actually "dislike" was too moderate a term, but I was trying to be diplomatic) that Grace felt for him, Mrs. Bailey walked in.

"Were you talking to him?" she asked.

"Oh, yes," I said. "I try to find the time to say something to him every day. It's marvelous how much he has responded, too, although I'll admit I don't understand him altogether when he tries to communicate with me."

She looked doubtful. "Well," she said, "that's something nobody else has tried, anyway."

Then she told me a lady who thought I was discharging her husband too soon was waiting to see me.

I spent the next fifteen minutes in one of the conference rooms listening to a small dark woman, who talked so much and so fast I wondered how she ever found out her husband was sick in the first place, tell me why she didn't want to take him home yet. She agreed that he seemed normal but that was exactly what made her uneasy because he hadn't been that way before he really got sick.

I sat waiting for a chance to speak when the conference room was filled with one of Mr. Peckham's messages.

Since I'd already accepted the fact of telepathy, transmission over a distance didn't seem so remarkable, but I was surprised at the effect it had on the woman. As though with the words of Mr. Peckman all about us there wasn't space for any more of hers, her voice slowed and stopped and then she said,

"All right, I'll take him home."

"What made you decide that?" I asked.

"I didn't," she said, "You did, but if you're so positive he'll be all right I guess he will."

The words had been "Serpent seventy" and I was on my way back to Mr. Peckham's room to acknowledge their receipt when I met Dr. Hahn.

"That was an excellent letter, Stephen."

"Thank you," I said, but he wanted to talk.

"I've always said, 'Handling the patient's relatives sometimes requires greater art than handling the patient.'"

"Yes, sir," I said.

"'—And can be fully as rewarding.'" I'd been in a hurry and interrupted a quotation.

111

"Yes, sir," I said.

"I'm going to ask a favor of you. I'd like you to present a patient at the next staff conference."

"Yes, sir," I said. I knew what was coming and couldn't see how to avoid it.

"How about this fellow you wrote the letter about? You said he was interesting."

"Very interesting," I said, and tried to get out of the trap I was in. "But not at all the kind of case that would be interesting for a staff conference. What I mean to say is that this case is interesting because it's so uninteresting. I guess I'd better take a few minutes to explain."

"No, never mind. I can wait till the conference. But it sounds ideal. Follow your own thinking as you went through the case, explain why you first thought it was unusual. Remember, we are here to train ["we"—not only was he using my first name, but now I was an assistant], and there is probably more to be gained from studying the commonplace illness that mimics the exotic than the reverse. I'm looking forward to it, Stephen."

Before I could find an answer, Dr. Hahn had turned and walked away.

I knew why he had asked me to present a case, and it was not altogether because I'd made the mistake of saying Mr. Peckham was one of the most interesting patients in the hospital. I'd accomplished something or played a major role in accomplishing something that was the gossip of the staff. Two people had been discharged in the past week, which wasn't so remarkable in itself, but the two had been more than patients, they were valuable employees; that their work had been called occupational therapy and their pay had been room and board and script honored at the commissary made them no less valuable. One had been an expert baker and the other had been virtually in charge of the laundry.

The combination in one morning of no starch in the uniforms and no blueberry muffins for coffee break had caused grumbling and then questions, and it was generally concluded that I was responsible, for I had been seeing them in weekly psychotherapy sessions.

When I explained to Mrs. Bailey that we should call what had happened remissions and not recoveries, she said that my humility was to be expected in one of truly great talent, that it was part of my "low-key approach" she'd noticed when I first came on the ward, and that it hadn't fooled her a bit. She was wrong: My "great talent" had been coming with the messages.

The patients involved had been veterans of so much therapy, including electric shock, the behavioral approach and psychoanalysis, with so little benefit that when I inherited them, treatment was continuing only to fulfill the requirements of state law. I had been restricted by my level of training to simple supportive psychotherapy (even this had been intermittent because of the demands of their work); still I had somehow dislodged them from their settled institutional life. I had encouraged and reassured them and denied their delusions, and when I had told them they would be better off outside, crowded in with their relatives and looking for work, I hadn't entirely believed it, but they had.

The two cases were only the most spectacular examples of the improvement in my work. When I conducted group therapy now I kept in control, not obviously either, but by directing through the members. And one of the couples I'd given counseling to had told me the wife was pregnant and the baby, if it were a boy, would be named after me. But I could never admit to anyone and especially not to the assembled staff how I'd gotten my ability or what Mr. Peckham was capable of otherwise.

If I presented Mr. Peckham without his power, what sort of conference would that be? There was the regular EBI (I wished that were a well-known test instead of one I'd thought up myself) and the consistent lab results. The presentation was supposed to last an hour, with fifteen minutes of that reserved for questions. Mr. Peckham without his special powers would not be enough. I'd have to ask Dr. Hahn to let me present the laundry worker or the baker.

29

A REMARK that Dr. Shields made helped me interpret the serpent message. It was his first day back at the hospital, and I had stopped him to offer my condolences.

"You have no idea how sorry I was to hear about your father," I said.

"Thanks. We knew there might be more trouble. This was his third attack."

Now I could ask a question I'd been wondering about since I'd last talked to him.

"Exactly when did it begin? When and how did the attack start?"

If Dr. Shields thought me morbid he didn't say so.

"There is no way to tell exactly. He was alone when it happened. When he was found he was unconscious, and he never came out of it. It could have been any time in the early afternoon."

"Was there an autopsy?"

"Oh, yes, it was his heart, all right."

"But if it was in the early afternoon, they should—" and then I stopped, for I had been about to ask, why couldn't they tell when it happened by how far his digestion of lunch had proceeded. But that was when it had started; he hadn't died until three days later.

Dr. Shields was waiting for me to finish.

"It all seems so damned unnecessary." I was repeating what I'd already said to Mr. Peckham because just a third attack would have let him keep his promise.

"You really do feel bad about it, don't you?" Then he changed the subject.

"I hear you are going to present Parsnip Peckham at a staff conference."

"Yes, and I wish I didn't have to."

"What do you mean, you wish you didn't have to? You lucky stiff. Why, I never heard of a first-year resident presenting a case. You'll have to tell me something about him so I can ask some good questions. It doesn't hurt to look sharp at those conferences. We can work out some questions and answers; it will make you look better too."

"Well," I said, "for one thing he has an absolutely precise EBI, eye-blink interval." And I began telling about eye-blinking and the purpose it served but stopped after a few words, for I was reading from page 1107 in a physiology text. That was the first time it happened when I'd had no alcohol.

"Go on, it sounds like you've got that cold."

I went on by memory, but the page was there if I'd wanted to refer to it. "The eye-blink interval is prolonged in hyperthyroidism, but I can't find any reference anywhere in the literature to a person with an invariably equal EBI."

"What else is there?"

"His lab work always comes out the same."

"What's so remarkable about that?"

"It's always the same—it hasn't varied in years."

"So what's the diagnosis?"

"The diagnosis, well, I guess, chronic deteriorated schizophrenia."

"Let's forget the question-and-answer routine; nobody is going to look good with this case."

"You don't think it's good enough for a conference."

"No; I tell you what: Tell them you are changing the format. This time, instead of asking questions if they want to, everyone has to ask a question. That will make about seventy questions, and you might make it last long enough."

Seventy, there were about that many on the staff. And they were medical people, so the serpent stood for the caduceus.

Dr. Shields went on, "Did you hear about the old G.P. who made a house call where a baby had a high fever? He looked the baby over and then he said to the mother, 'Well, I don't know if I can help, I ain't so good with fevers—but I can give him something that will give him fits, and I'm great on fits.'

"That's what you should do. Give him something to cause fits and then tell them how you cured the fits."

"Don't ever say such a thing!"

Dr. Shields looked around because I'd whispered.

"O.K. So it wasn't a good joke, but it was just a joke."

Then he said, "I hear you are seeing Grace tonight."

It was a package deal, I thought, and you lose.

"Yes, I guess so," I said.

"I couldn't get her to understand," he said, "that God wouldn't have made her that good-looking if He hadn't expected her to put out."

We saw Grace walking toward us then and I thought again of my unbelievable luck that hadn't been luck at all.

"Were you talking about me?" she asked.

"We were comparing notes," Dr. Shields said.

"He hasn't had time for notes," she said to him.

"Mostly we have been talking about eye-blinking," I said.

"Well, if you aren't talking about me, just about everyone else is."

"Why is that?" Dr. Shields asked.

"Dr. Kildare here had to let everyone know where they could reach him, at a moment's notice so he gave the afternoon nurse my phone number. Now everyone knows, all right. He might as well have put it on the Goodyear Blimp that he was sleeping with me."

"I'm sorry about that," I said.

Dr. Shields looked stunned. "Christ, whatever you are, don't be sorry," he said.

"Let's make rounds now," she said to Dr. Shields, "and you can get acquainted with your patients again."

As they walked away I thought how nice they looked together.

30

"DON'T GET the wrong idea about Dr. Shields."

It was the next morning and I was talking to Mr. Peckham. "He's irreverent and high-spirited and was only joking. Heaven knows—well, he has had his share of trouble.

"I've been wondering, too, what good warnings are if I can't figure out what it means until after the trouble happens?

"And whether or not I interpreted that correctly about the seventy snakes, what do I do now? Do you want me to expose you to all these people? If that is what you really want, you are going about it all wrong. Believe me, without some demonstration on your part, like sending a message to everyone about fifteen minutes into that conference, if I tell everything, I'll just end up where you are. This may be a perfect arrangement for you—"

The next message came: "Twins twelve." It was what I'd been waiting for. I left then and went about my regular work.

I'd planned the trip to Merri Hours for that afternoon, but I didn't get there.

Grace's parents were coming to visit her and she had told me I would have to stay in the residents' hall that night. By one-thirty I was almost ready to leave for the nursing home when Grace led me aside.

They never stayed longer than a couple of hours and couldn't I read a book in the bedroom while they were there? I agreed without telling her of the unpleasant chore I'd postponed.

When the doorbell rang that evening I took a textbook with me into the bedroom. It was a pleasant room and no more cluttered by two people's things than it had been with one's. I was moving clothes from the chair to the bed when Grace opened the door.

"Someone wants to see you."

I followed her into the living room where two men were waiting. If they were twins they weren't identical twins. They didn't look more alike than any two college tackles might fifteen years after graduation or any two detectives might.

That's it, I thought. They were sent here by Mr. Waggoner, and though my being in the bedroom may be difficult to explain, they were here too early for real evidence.

"Dr. Boyd." The one who spoke was heavier by ten pounds and carried a briefcase.

"There is a gentleman who is a patient of yours, an Ernest Peckham."

"Yes."

"We represent an insurance company. Many years ago a disability policy was written on him. Even though it isn't much per month, over the years that it has been in force the company has paid out a considerable sum. We would like to know, what are his prospects of recovery?"

"You want to know if he will get well and will be able to or will function normally?" I asked.

"Yes."

"He won't; there is no chance of that."

"We understand he has improved and that he's talking. What is the nature of his improvement, and what exactly is he saying?"

He took a notebook from his pocket.

"May I sit down?" he asked and sat on the davenport.

"I can't tell you anything." And then, because I'd never seen anything about insurance on any of Mr. Peckham's records, I said, "Even if you were insurance people, which I doubt, I can't tell you anything. Patients' communications are privileged."

They looked at each other, and the one standing by the door spoke for the first time, "It's best to tell us, it will save all of us trouble."

It wasn't what he said but his manner that alarmed me. He was nervous and expected trouble.

Grace walked toward the door but he backed ahead of her and stood in front of it.

"There are people coming," she said, "they will be here in a few minutes. You will both have to go now."

"Isn't that the way it always is?" The man on the couch still had his notebook open. "You're here by yourselves all alone and cozy for twelve nights in a row and all at once everybody's got to come barging in."

The three of us stood and watched as he seemed to doodle in his notebook. Then he went on.

"I understand he's been balmy for years, so what's the harm in telling us what he's saying?"

"I could make up anything," I said. "You wouldn't know."

"Yes, why don't you do that?" The man by the door plainly wanted to finish here and leave.

"Shut up," the one who was sitting said in the same reasonable voice.

"Steve, what difference can it make? Tell them and maybe they will go," Grace said.

In high school, while I was waiting for a spurt of growth that never came, when I was overmatched I used to pretend to know karate. Since my residency, though, I had worked out what I thought was a better plan. Whether the peculiar dread that people feel for the lunatic is conditioned by stories heard in childhood or whether it is instinctive and fostered in the species by selection, it is greater than the fear engendered by a reasonable person trained in a scientific method of fighting.

After the initial footwork and shout it had always been obvious that I knew nothing about karate, but now with my training I could mimic insanity indefinitely.

"Twelve twins," I shouted.

"What?" He closed his notebook.

"Seventy snakes," I shouted again.

He stood up.

"Sixty-eight foxes," and then I lapsed into the most startling manifestation of a psychosis I had ever seen, Mr. Sedges' secret language. Growling and barking, I advanced.

The man at the door had left when I'd called up the foxes,

and now the other, holding his briefcase in front of him with both hands and watching me warily, backed across the room. He turned and ran the last few steps and I followed in full cry, out the door and partway down the hall.

When I turned back I saw for the first time that a man and woman had stepped aside to let the procession out.

I hurried by them back into the bedroom and closed the door.

31

MOMENTS LATER Grace came into the bedroom again.

"There's no other way, you will have to come out now."

She led me back to the living room and introduced me to her parents. Their name was Holmes. He was tall and dark with thick graying hair and a neatly trimmed mustache. She was slightly overweight and her features were too coarse, I thought, for her to ever have been as beautiful as her daughter.

I shook his hand and remembered too late that I have been criticized for a limp grip.

"You shouldn't get the wrong impression," I said, "I was just trying to frighten those men."

Mrs. Holmes said, "Of course," and looked at her daughter.

"Don't worry, mother," Grace sat down on the couch. "He has had all his shots."

I told them about the visitors who had refused to leave.

"Maybe they would have left if we had just yelled or made a commotion," I said, "but I'm sure it's more unnerving when someone acts completely psychotic."

"I think that is so true," Mrs. Holmes said.

Mr. Holmes said, "I suppose you could get carried away doing a thing like that."

His wife thought we ought to call the police at once, and while we were waiting for them we should all have a drink. "I just can't believe you made those dreadful noises," she said.

"I don't want anything to drink," I said.

"Don't you ever imbibe?" Mr. Holmes asked.

"I'll have a beer, and I'd like it out of the can."

Mrs. Holmes helped Grace with the drinks, and in spite of what I'd said brought me my can of beer with part of it poured in a glass.

As we talked, I pretended to drink now and then from the can.

Mr. Holmes asked me what was the difference between a real M.D. and a psychiatrist and what a resident was.

I explained this to him and he said, "When Gracie said you were a psychiatric resident at the state hospital and with you barking like that I thought she had brought home some of her work." He had a hearty laugh.

"I'm just an ordinary businessman," he said. "I have a fuel oil company, but I don't mind telling you I could never buy this Freud crap. It's just high-class pornography."

"He was changing his theories all the time," I said. "If he were alive now he probably wouldn't buy it all either."

Mrs. Holmes asked if I analyzed dreams and did I believe in telepathy, and Mr. Holmes asked when I'd be going into practice.

Two policemen came and we told our stories again. They took the address and telephone number of Mr. Peckham's sister and were going to go to the hospital and interview Mr. Peckham the next day, but I told them that would be useless.

While the policemen were leaving, I tried to get some of the beer in my glass poured back in the can. Mr. Holmes caught me at it and nudged his wife.

"I like beer better out of a can," I explained. Then because they had the look again of people examining a specimen, I took a small sip out of the glass.

"What's in your pocket?" Mr. Holmes asked.

"It's a fountain pen," and I handed him the big black Ink-O-Graph I had been carrying.

Years ago, the first owner of that pen had had his name,

Stephen Ellender, engraved on it. Mr. Holmes noticed this at once.

"I thought Stephen Boyd was a phony name," he said. "Are you even a doctor?"

I explained that I collected pens, that some of them had names on them, and that most of the people who first owned them had been dead for years.

"Why, I think that is a fascinating hobby," Mrs. Holmes said.

"Let me give you some pens that won't get ink on your fingers," Mr. Holmes said and he handed me two ball-point pens that had "Holmes is where the heat is" printed on them.

He started telling me about the car he had bought only the week before. It had steel-belted rubber all around, a four-barrel carburetor, and an eight-to-one compression ratio. No one could beat him from a light because he could go from standing still to sixty miles per hour in ten seconds.

I made comments now and then like, "That's what I call carburetion," and "That's a ratio."

Grace and her mother were talking about women's lib, but now Grace interrupted us. "He doesn't drive, Dad."

Mr. Holmes said, "You mean none of what I told you means anything to you at all?"

I said, "Well, that start is a full second faster than what a 1914 Stanley Steamer could do," and realized the memory trouble had started again.

There had been a pro football game that day on TV and he asked me if I'd seen it. When I said I hadn't, he asked if I knew anything about football. I told him it had once been a game to play primarily as a part of the Shrove Tuesday Festival. Then everybody played, all ages and both sexes, and I thought this was a more wholesome arrangement than the one they had now.

Mr. Holmes didn't say anything, but Mrs. Holmes said that was fascinating, and what did I think of women's lib?

"It's women's reaction to the trials placed on them by the universal latent homosexuality among men," I said.

"Christ," Mr. Holmes said, and his face had gotten red. "He's not a doctor becoming a psychiatrist, he's a fruit turning into a nut."

"Your agitation at what I have said and your liking pro football illustrate very aptly a statement of Freud's: 'Those objects to which men give their preference originate in the same perceptions and experiences as those objects of which they have the most abhorrence.'"

Mrs. Holmes said, "We should be leaving now. Can we drop you off somewhere, Dr. Boyd?"

"Like a bridge," her husband said.

"No, I want him to stay a few minutes," Grace said. "I've got something to say to him."

Her mother said, "I hope you don't make the same mistake again, dear."

"Don't worry, I won't," Grace said.

As soon as the door closed, she turned on me.

"I should have left you in the bedroom."

"I like you much better than your parents."

"You didn't have to say what you did. You're not going to cure any complexes this late at night. And you know it. I think you're a big—I just about called you a big prick, you little prick."

"Well, you didn't help any when you said I couldn't drive. That's when things really started to go sour." But I knew it hadn't been her fault. It was the sip of beer that had expanded my memory so much I couldn't pick out the right thing to say.

"What did your mother mean," I asked, "when she said you shouldn't make the same mistake again?"

"She thinks I don't charge enough."

I laughed and started toward her, but she backed away.

"There's nothing wrong with my parents, you're the misfit screwball, you know that, don't you?"

"Succinct succubus," I said, and reached for her but she dodged and ran into the bedroom.

I followed her in time to help her drag the chair over in front of the closet. When she climbed on the chair and reached to the back of a shelf, I steadied her at first and then tried to reach the top of her panty hose.

She twisted away and we nearly fell into the closet. Regaining my balance, I stepped back and was hit in the face with my paper bag. It broke and the contents—pajamas, towel, tooth-brush, razor, and a paperback sex manual with many loose pages —scattered behind me.

"Take your silly sack and pack your suitcases—your education is finished here," she said.

I began gathering my belongings from the floor.

"The resolution of a quarrel often results in heightened sexual pleasure," I said, selecting a passage from the manual that I now could have quoted from cover to cover and even included the two misprints.

She watched me for a moment in silence. "That's a great idea; now hurry up and get out of here so I can call my husband."

"You won't be able to do that," I said, "it's useless to try."

"What do you know about him?" she asked.

"Nothing; I'm talking about you: You are stuck with me, even more so than for better or for worse."

"If there is one thing I know, it's that I can have anyone I want," she said.

Perhaps she could have once, I thought, but now as a swan whether she knew it or not she was permanently monogamous.

I was arranging the pages of my manual in order when the phone rang and she went to answer it.

32

OUT IN the living room, I began looking through the records for Grace's favorite.

"I don't want to hear that now," she said.

I sat by her on the davenport.

"It's crazy. That call was about Gerry—he's been hurt in an auto accident."

"Who's Gerry?" I asked, though I'd already guessed who he was.

"Oh, Gerry, he's the person I married once. What's crazy is I don't think I've thought of him in days, and then I mention him and this call comes. I guess I'd better tell you about him."

She had met him when she'd been in training. At first, he was just another patient, but then one day when she had the job of checking through his things (this was done regularly when he was out of his room because he had been hospitalized after a suicide attempt), she'd found a dozen drawings of her. He was an artist; he was handsome and intelligent, but most of all he had a great and careless talent as an artist.

She supposed her attitude changed toward him after she found the pictures. In those days when she was first starting in psychiatry she had been naïve and thought that everyone got well who wanted to and accepted treatment.

Their meeting, after he was discharged, seemed like an accident, but later he admitted that he had arranged it. There was a frantic courtship of six weeks, and during that time she was wonderfully happy and he seemed so completely well she almost forgot how they had met. The marriage, if you could call it that, had lasted six weeks, too.

Nasal congestion had changed her voice, and I got her some Kleenex.

The boy who had everything couldn't have an erection—at least not with her. She had learned what she called her bedroom acrobatics trying to interest him. They tried everything until one night he came home and coaxed her to try one thing more. When she realized she had been going to do it, had been going to do it without question just because it was the next logical step, she threw whatever was in reach and drove them out, for Gerry had brought home a friend.

"Like a TV audience he wanted to watch a warmup session and then he was going to come on strong for the main bill and, as he put it, 'take wet deck.'"

She hadn't seen him since, but there had been letters. At first, they had been part apology and part pornography, and then he'd started psychotherapy again and they had gotten better and sounded more like the person she'd known before she had married.

"That call was from a friend who was with him. I guess Gerry was on his way back here to see me." She blew her nose again. "The sad, sad son-of-a-bitch," she said.

"How did it happen?" I asked. "Was anyone else hurt?"

"It was a freakish accident: They were taking turns driving and Gerry was asleep in the back seat. Something went wrong with the car and they stopped at a service station. Gerry woke up and tried to get out when it was up on one of those racks. He's unconscious. His friend didn't know anything about us— he thought I ought to come.

"And so now you know," she said, "why I wasn't upset with your 'nemertean' quickie. I found it refreshing after Gerry. And when I said I was going to call him I was just trying to hurt you; I don't know why."

Mr. Waggoner's mother called the next night. He had fractured his skull and had had an operation but wasn't any better.

After Grace hung up the phone, she walked about the apartment with her arms folded across her chest as if she were cold.

"She says it's my duty now to come. I'm not going to. She says I'm the only person he's ever loved. He never loved me; he wanted me to cure him. She says I never knew how fond she was of me. She hated me before she'd even seen me."

Night after night the calls came.

The morning after we had heard of the accident I'd gone in to Mr. Peckham's room, and instead of talking aloud had tried telepathy. I was appalled at his callous attitude about people. My relationship with Grace was sound enough that I didn't need more help, not the drastic kind of help he gave, anyway. He alone was responsible for what had happened; certainly I'd not expected anyone to be injured or lose their lives.

But in spite of my efforts to concentrate on my message, I began to wonder, was I entirely honest? Would I trade my knack for psychotherapy and Grace to have those people alive and well that I'd never seen? I was glad I didn't have to choose. I'd spoken or rather thought my piece and for once, perhaps, I'd gotten an answer.

The interval between the messages had been getting shorter; only four days after "Twins twelve" another, "Painter twenty-five," came.

It's hard to say how long a message lasted. Each began at a maximum intensity that was maintained a few seconds, then it faded rapidly but not completely, so that there was no way to know exactly when it was gone. It's as if you struck a tuning fork and induced vibration in another fork by holding them close. You couldn't tell by listening whether the sound from the first had stopped and you were hearing only the second one.

Again I wasn't near Mr. Peckham but in a conference room at the other end of the ward. A man with a postoperative psychosis was explaining to me why he had been hiding all of his things in the most unlikely places he could think of. Scientists had gotten his appendix and by cloning (a process he had heard of on the TV talk shows) were growing thousands of people just like him, but he'd be able to prove he was the original: They wouldn't know where his things were hidden.

Before the message had faded, I directed a plea toward the room at the end of the hall asking that the young artist be spared. I wasn't able to find out if it was too late even then.

That evening, the last call came. He had died that day. I kept asking Grace to find out exactly when it happened, but she was upset and wasn't listening to me.

She was crying when she hung up the phone.

"She was just terrible. She says it's my fault it happened in the first place and if I had come and held his hand he would have known I was there and gotten well. She says he spent his last hours calling for me. Do you believe that?"

It was possible, I supposed, but there was only one answer.

"No," I said.

"I was going to go, I suppose, if this had kept on. Now I wish I had."

"You couldn't have helped," I said. "His mother is the one who is to blame if anybody is. I was afraid this might happen when she kept calling."

"What do you mean?" she asked.

"Just from what you told me about how he was," I lied. "I knew

127

he couldn't get well when he showed no improvement after the operation."

"Is that right?"

"Absolutely," I said. "And I'm particularly sure there is no way you could have helped or that he would have known you."

If she had tried to go, it would have only ended sooner, but there was no way to tell her that. What I had said, though, seemed to have helped her.

"Come along and I'll show you what I meant when I said he was talented."

Down in the basement storeroom she picked out four pictures from a stack leaning against the wall. We carried them up to the apartment and set them about the living room.

I said they were good. Perhaps they were even great. In three of them, he had used an economy of line that suggested far more. The fourth was a watercolor of Grace in the nude and was done in photographic detail.

"He worked on that off and on the whole time we were married," she said, "in more ways than one."

He hadn't caught her, though. The woman in the picture was Grace, but a Grace that faintly resembled her mother.

Sometime later she said, "Just a second," and stepped across the room to turn a picture to the wall. I realized that the thin, handsome young man on the canvas had been the twenty-five-year-old painter.

33

I BOUGHT A CHAIN LOCK for the apartment so that we wouldn't have to open the door for everyone who rang the bell.

While I was installing it Grace said again, "I just can't understand why anyone would be interested in Mr. Peckham."

She sat with her feet curled under her. A cup of coffee was balanced beside her on the arm of the couch and a *House Beautiful* magazine was open on her lap.

It would have been a relief for me to tell her everything. I was tired of my secret but I couldn't share it because there was no way to make her believe it.

"Anyone who is connected with a wealthy family is likely to get attention one way or another," I said.

"What is that supposed to mean?"

"Maybe they were thinking of blackmail."

"That's silly. He's been in a public hospital for years."

"Maybe they were newspaper reporters."

"If they were, they passed up a better story: 'Doctor turns werewolf.'"

"Do you know something about all this you haven't told me?" she asked then.

"Well," I said, "I think Mr. Peckham's brother-in-law, perhaps because of money, doesn't want him to get well."

"He's got nothing to worry about, then," she said.

It was a good lock but I knew that either of the two men could have pushed in the flimsy door. Perhaps the lack of soundproofing protected us, because they never visited our apartment again.

One day about noon (I say about noon but it was thirty-two seconds after eleven fifty-three when Mrs. Bailey called me to the phone) Dr. Adler telephoned me.

He had reconsidered, he said, and he believed he could be of some help to me after all. Would it be all right if his driver picked me up at seven that evening and brought me out to his home for a conference? I agreed and gave him the address of the apartment.

A few minutes later, there was another message from Mr. Peckham. I was in the cafeteria line, which meant that it came through three floors of a concrete building, the farthest of any so far. For the first time a word was repeated; it was "Eagle," with the number "eighteen." I moved along and chose my food with the others. They were completely unaware of what had happened.

That afternoon on our way home, I told Grace about the telephone call and asked if she wanted to come, too.

"It will be fun," she said, "riding in a car as a passenger. I suppose there is no need to ask who you're going to talk about. It's Mr. Mushroom again."

"Yes." I wished she wouldn't say that.

"Is he really going to be presented at a staff conference?"

"I guess so; maybe I'll find out something about him tonight that will be helpful."

"I can't see how a person who just lies in bed could be so repulsive."

"You shouldn't—" I began.

"I know, I know. But that is the way I feel."

The driver who rang the bell of the apartment at three minutes to seven wore a chauffeur's uniform, including the billed cap. We followed him downstairs and found waiting in the passenger-loading zone a long, low, black, foreign-made car. It was completely black. If it had ever had any chrome, this had been painted black, too.

The driver held the door for us while we got in. What must have been taped music was playing softly. The seats were of soft black leather and the trim about the windows was rosewood polished to a dull sheen. A glass partition separated us from the chauffeur.

Grace said, "I've seen this whole thing on "The Late Show." Shall I tell you what's going to happen, or do you want to wait and see for yourself?"

The music was interrupted by a voice. "If you'd like a drink, you'll find everything in the cupboard in front of you."

I saw the driver replace a small speaker on the dashboard.

"How about one for the road?" Grace asked.

She leaned forward and slid back a louvered door and there, fitted into shelves behind it, were cut glass decanters, glasses, and bottles.

"Not for me," I said.

"You haven't seen the show," and she began making a drink for herself.

We entered the freeway and headed north out of the city.

Grace lifted a small speaker from a cradle in front of us.

"I think I'll tell him to kick this buggy in the ass and we'll see what it can do."

"I'm not allowed to go over the speed limit, ma'am." It was the driver again.

"Oh, well," Grace stretched out her legs and leaned back in the seat. "I'll tell you how this turns out. We drive out to a castle. In the basement is a laboratory where this doctor, that's Boris Karloff, with a trained idiot as an assistant is going to exchange your brain and Mr. Peckham's. Now would you like a drink?"

I pointed to the driver. "Maybe he can hear us."

"If they know we are onto them they just might cancel it."

We took an exit into a prosperous middle-class suburb.

"This place wasn't in the movie," Grace said.

But we didn't stop. The street we were on became narrower as we left town until finally we were on a two-lane asphalt road that wound up into forested hills. Here and there an entrance gate marked where a driveway led back into the trees, and now and then we glimpsed architectural details of houses that were a quarter of a mile away.

Finally, twenty-two minutes and eight seconds after leaving the freeway, we turned off the road and waited while ornate wrought-iron gates opened in front of us. At first, the way was very steep; then it became more gradual, and we came out of the trees about 212—pardon—two hundred yards from the road.

In front of us on the rounded top of what was the highest elevation for many miles was a house with crenelated walls of rough brick, deep narrow windows, and a circular tower on one corner. A lawn sloped down for fifty yards to the trees. On either side of us topiaries of birds and animals formed a procession that led up to the house. When we got out of the car, I saw in the center of a circle made by the driveway a huge boxwood bird with curved beak and half-spread wings.

We climbed five wide steps that were made to look like a drawbridge by heavy iron chain railings. The massive door of dark oak was arch-shaped and had for a knocker an eagle that dropped its beak on a cowering fawn.

"Maybe we had better just make a run for it now," Grace said. "I'd rather take my chances with the dogs."

"What dogs?" I asked.

"I keep forgetting, you didn't see that show."

A maid opened the door and led us to a library that looked like what I imagined a smaller reading room in an exclusive gentleman's club might.

Dr. Adler came in by another door. He was tall and slim and looked no more than fifty, though I knew he must be much older. His hair was blond and longer than any M.D. except a psychiatrist would have allowed.

We had finished introductions when Mrs. Adler came in. She was much younger than her husband and a beautiful woman, though she had begun the redistribution of tissue from her extremities to her torso characteristic of the alcoholic.

After more introductions, his wife offered to "entertain your lovely young lady while you men have your talk." There must not have been a Mrs. Adler in the movie, for Grace left without a backward glance.

After I refused a drink and a cigar and we were settled in soft leather chairs, Dr. Adler began.

"Well, there has been a change in Ernest Peckham."

"He's talking," I said. This was not exactly true, but all I could admit until I had an indication that Dr. Adler expected more.

"What has he said?"

I repeated each message and the date I'd received it, and Dr. Adler copied this into a small notebook he carried.

"Have you made any sense out of this?"

"Some of the combinations could be stock quotations." I laughed and continued, "Some could be interpreted as intelligent tips on the market."

Dr. Adler looked up at me. His eyes I saw now were remarkably blue. Then he studied the list again.

"This proves anyone can make money in a bull market. Does he ever look at a newspaper?"

"He is often in a day room where there are papers, but he appears unaware of everything about him."

"Have you started a new medicine or treatment?"

"No, but I am sure that I'm talking to him more than anyone else has. At least for several years," I added.

"The speech is typical of a schizophrenic. What is amazing is that it has begun after all these years of silence."

"Can you tell me more about his childhood?" I asked and I told him what I'd learned from the hospital chart.

"I'm afraid I can't add much to that," Dr. Adler said. "You see, my sole source of information was a sister who has been psychotic intermittently for years. What she told me varied from the fantastic to the outright delusional. For instance: that he talked in sentences at six months, that he was reading before he was a year old, that no school could be found for him because of his brilliance, and even that he quit talking only because he was able to communicate by telepathy."

I made a mistake then, not so much because I was excited (after all, I'd guessed some time ago most of what he had told me) but because I was wondering what it had been like as a member of that family when young Peckham first began to experiment with his unique talent.

So when Dr. Adler said, "If you won't have a drink, how about a cup of coffee with a spot of brandy in it?" I was preoccupied and accepted.

"The truth is," Dr. Adler continued, "that, as is not unusual in childhood schizophrenia, he was precocious, could not adapt to school, and the disease when it began followed a pernicious course."

"What do you know about the accident that killed his parents?"

"Now, that is where I can give you some information, for that was no accident at all."

The maid brought us coffee, and when Dr. Adler poured some brandy in mine I could have refused it and asked for another cup, but I thought that it would call less attention to my idiosyncrasy if I simply did not drink it. This was another mistake.

"That fire," Dr. Adler said, "was not an accident but was set. It's all ancient history now and you are concerned in the case, so I will tell you, in confidence, of course, that it was planned as a murder and double suicide and turned out because of the heroism of Ernest's brother-in-law to be only a double suicide.

"How can you be sure of that?" I put the coffee cup to my lips and set it down again. I didn't have to pretend; it was too hot to drink.

"There is no doubt about that. You see, they left a note."

"Have you seen it?"

"No, but I've been told what was in it, and it was authentic. They even sent an additional note to the insurance company so that a double indemnity accident policy would not be paid. They were so wealthy that their honesty caused no hardship for their heirs. The note is interesting, for it emphasizes the heritable nature of the disease. The Peckhams believed that their unfortunate child was a monster that had to be exterminated."

I pretended to sip my coffee.

"I'll confess," he continued, "that my purpose in bringing you here was not to discuss a case that your most enthusiastic efforts can only make less of a nursing problem. I wanted to talk of your plans for yourself.

"Your concern for this patient impressed me so favorably I took the liberty of checking your credentials. Believe me, you can do far better than continue in what I'm afraid is a distinctly second-rate residency. Resign there at once. I've already arranged for your appointment at the Bollinger Clinic, which is, as you know, the most prestigious psychiatric facility in the United States, or more correctly, the world. When you finish in two and a half years (I've also arranged that you'll get credit for the time you've already spent in residency), you'll come in with me as a full partner. I'll postpone retirement until you are established, and then you can take over my practice, and as you can see, it has provided for me very comfortably."

I looked about me at the rows of books, the marble fireplace, and the Tiffany lamps.

"Is there something wrong with your coffee?" he asked.

134

"No," I said, and pretended to sip.

"I've contacted Dr. Hahn who, by the way, has given you the highest recommendations and has agreed to release you from your commitments at the state hospital. As a matter of fact, you won't need to return there. They expect you at Bollinger within a week, so you will be busy with packing for the next few days."

He paused and I finally had a chance to ask, "What about Samuel Holden, the orderly?"

"Who?"

"Samuel Holden, the orderly who was the reason for Mr. Peckham leaving the sanitarium?"

"Oh, yes, I remember something of that. He was a borderline psychotic himself. If the young lady you brought here is an important part of your plans, I will arrange for her to join the staff of the clinic."

I didn't answer immediately and he said,

"I'll need to know shortly in order to get an additional plane reservation."

"I am flattered," I said, "at the confidence you place in me, but I won't be able to leave. You can cancel the reservation altogether." If I were going to desert Mr. Peckham, I certainly wouldn't fly away in a plane.

"I'm prepared," Dr. Adler said, "to put my offer of partnership in a written contract."

"I don't need," I said, "even time to think it over. I'm engaged in a sort of research project now. If your offer is still in effect in six months, perhaps I can accept then."

"Come with me," he said. "I'll show you about the house."

I soon recognized a pattern in Dr. Adler's conducting of the tour, and I cooperated. He would stop before a picture, a sculpture, or a piece of furniture and describe it briefly. We looked at it until I made a comment of appreciation, and then we moved on.

But before we got out of the library, a slight break occurred in the ritual.

"This stained-glass table lamp in a dragonfly pattern was designed by Tiffany and is signed on the base and shade," Dr. Adler said.

"It's beautiful," I answered, "but was designed by Clara Driscoll, a woman in his employ. She won a a prize with this at the Paris Exposition of 1903."

This was conversation, even small-talk, made with assurance, and I was unaware that it was an extraordinary thing to have said.

Dr. Adler hesitated and then led me on to the next room. In a picture gallery, he stopped before a small painting, a landscape that included ancient buildings and a bridge.

"This is a priceless Guardi. He was an eighteenth-century Italian."

"Francesco, Giacomo, or Giovanni?" I asked.

"You have a fantastic knowledge of art," he said.

"It's spotty," I said, "and is confined to artists rather than art." I had become so sensitive to alcohol that the peculiar reaction had been precipitated by the fumes of the brandy. Fifteen years ago, I had looked in an encyclopedia for guillotine, the subject of a seventh-grade report, and now I knew from a description on a page I had glanced at and turned by then the details of an obsure family of artists. After that, like a spy who might betray himself with a remark, I mentally checked my sources before I said anything.

There was only one lapse brought on because I became too interested in one of Dr. Adler's showpieces, a heavy carved chest with brass ormolu and a marble top. As usual, Dr. Adler quoted its pedigree. When I didn't respond, he said,

"You have a connoisseur's sense for fine craftsmanship."

"That fossil crinoid in the marble," I said, "is undoubtedly an Uintacrinus from the Cretaceous system."

Once we came out on a terrace and saw below us, surrounded by a capsule of light, Grace and Mrs. Adler in swimming suits sitting beside a tiled pool.

"Your friend would fit well in a setting such as this," Dr. Adler said.

I refused a game of billiards in a room with three tables and the fourth fireplace I had seen and then, the tour over, we went back to the library.

"I'm not offering you this," Dr. Adler said, "but in a few years you'll be easily able to afford its equivalent if you'll change your residency."

"I still can't accept."

"Are you one of these young people who aren't interested in material things?"

"I don't want to own them."

"Nobody owns them. I am a custodian who has made a deposit to insure that I will take good care of all this. Someday, if I have discharged my responsibilities well, the deposit will be returned and will be multiplied several times. Meanwhile I enjoy it all."

He didn't look like he was enjoying himself. I didn't say anything.

"What is distressing is that you're giving it up for the most pointless reason. I tell you that man is and always will be nothing more than a deteriorated schizophrenic."

He had finally raised his voice.

"Yes, sir," I said.

Grace, her face shining and her dark wet hair coiled up on her head, joined us then, and thirty-three seconds later, Mrs. Adler came in.

As soon as we were back in the car, Grace asked, "Well, are we flying back to the Midwest?"

"No, not unless you can talk some sense into me in the next ten days."

"Did you get to go through the house?"

"Yes," I said. "There's a fortune in art and antique furniture in there."

"There's another fortune in liquor hidden in the antique furniture."

"How did you like the house?" I asked.

She moved over against me and I put my arm around her.

"How would I know?" she said. "I didn't get to see the bedrooms."

34

DURING THE NIGHT the phone rang. I went out in the living room to answer it.

"Dr. Boyd?" a woman asked.

"Yes."

"Could you come down to Apartment 10 right away? There is a man here—I think he is dead." She sounded upset.

"Yes," I said.

Back in the bedroom and too sleepy to hurry, I began dressing.

"Is it the hospital?" Grace asked.

"No. Someone wants me to see someone downstairs."

She sat up. "See who downstairs?"

"Someone is sick or dead maybe," I said. "It was a woman in Apartment 10 who called. I'll be right back."

"That's the manager," she said. "How did they know you were a doctor?"

I wondered too how they knew my name.

I had to hold the banister and feel my way down the last of the stairs because the lights were out in the hall below and over the door to the outside. I turned in the direction of the manager's apartment and was grabbed from behind in a bear hug.

The first blow glanced along my jaw and made my mouth bleed; the next dazed me with an explosion of pale blue light. After that they hit me each time so hard in my middle I would have bent over if I weren't held up. When some ribs broke I thought it the worst pain I'd ever felt until another punch landed in the same place.

The person behind me let go and I was held up by my hair while a wad of paper was stuffed in my mouth. They pushed me to the floor and I lay rolled up in a ball waiting for a kick that didn't come. When the door slammed I got to my feet and pulled myself along the banister up the stairs.

Grace was waiting for me in the living room.

"Stephen! What's happened? Did you fall downstairs again?"

"I was beat up."

"Look at your poor eye! Who did it?"

"I don't know. It was dark down there. Someone was waiting for me."

While she got ice for my eye I looked at the paper they had stuffed in my mouth. It was wet with blood and saliva, and the heading had been cut off so there was no margin at the top, but my signature was at the bottom. It was the letter I'd written to Mr. Vukov.

I got out of calling the police that night by saying I was too sick to wait up and talk to them. The next morning I said I would after Grace had gone to work, but I didn't.

I took four days off to recover, but on the last day instead of staying home I set out for Merri Hours.

35

ON THE BUS when, by direct line, I was over twenty-three miles from the hospital, a message came. The distance had no effect on its intensity, but the affect component had undergone a complete reversal in polarity.

With my head aching like this and the pain in my side almost as bad as it ever had been, why hadn't I stayed home in bed?

That's where I should be, shut somewhere in a room for weeks yet, maybe forever. It was a pointless trip anyway, one lunatic investigating another; if I could gather the energy I'd get off the bus and turn back.

What had been scratches in the paint on the seat ahead of me I saw were obscene drawings. And the armrest, where had the thousands of hands gathered the filth that was compacted there? On the way to my seat how had I missed stepping on the bolus of phlegm? Some bronchitic invalid had gouged a huge blob from his lungs and, weakened by his spasm of coughing, had managed only enough force to give it a partial revolution after its impact with the floor. Grime that had rolled up on the glistening surface gave it an unusual cartographic pattern.

The passengers, listless subhuman hominoids, too preoccupied in depravity to recognize their stage in dying, shuffled by on their way to the rear door where, like extrusions from a mechanical cloaca, they were deposited along our way.

When it was my turn and I left the bus there was no relief outside.

Later as part of my preparation for the staff conference I went back and looked at that neighborhood again and found it was not as down-at-the-heels as some other places I've seen. But that morning the decaying houses epitomized the futility of mankind's efforts for permanence.

Only the litter, the by-product of a culture's bizarre dedication to creating appetites, would last. It spilled over from front yards and vacant lots across the sidewalk and into the street where, ground to a finer texture but still indestructible, it was thrown up on the sidewalk again. Thus walking on a terrace of rubbish, I came to Merri Hours. It was a big old Victorian house, dead from a hole in the side.

Located somewhere else it could have become the headquarters of a county historical society, but here it had been abandoned to Mrs. Hatch or someone like her. That entrepreneur had built a wide stairway up the side and had cut through the elaborate pattern of shingles into the second floor.

I went up a ramp that had replaced the front steps and, obeying the signs on the door, walked in.

The horror I felt was not for the creatures I found there or for the fecal smell they lay in like shrimps in a marinade. What filled me with unutterable despair was the pointlessness of their experience, which had eventually returned them, alone and unaware of it, to the mindless state of infancy. Somewhere, muffled by the oppressive atmosphere, a voice began calling into a particular past for Mildred.

Avoiding hands that reached for any movement, I edged between beds and wheelchairs past a white marble fireplace like a cross section of a giant bone. Deep in the interior I found her in a circle of light that lit up rows of metal charts and made her eyes gleam under her dyed hair.

"I'm Dr. Boyd," I said.

"You have come so early, you have caught us before we've had a chance for our morning tidy-up."

"Are you Mrs. Hatch?"

"Yes, I want you to know that though we may not have the stainless steel gadgets some of your new places have, we make up for it with love and affection. Did you want to send someone here?"

"I want to talk about Mr. Peckham."

Her tongue came out between tiny, pointed teeth, wet her lips, and vanished again.

"I've told you all I know; you've wasted your time. Now, I'm busy."

"I'm going to send him back."

"Well, I won't accept him. He made too much noise."

"More than him?" I said when the voice cried out again for Mildred.

"Yes, more than him," she said, and the tongue darted over the lips again.

When she suddenly blinked twice, my feeling of revulsion unaccountably increased.

"What did he say to you?" I tried to make my voice more resonant in imitation of the messages.

"I won't say. I don't remember; I've got work to do." The tongue darted out and she blinked again, slowly. This time I saw the lower lids rise and cover but not completely obscure the shiny eyes.

"What did he say to you, Doctor?" she asked.

I moved back a step. "Hercules thirty-four," I said.

She watched me and blinked again in her strange way.

"Lizard thirty-six." It was the message I had received on the bus, and I shouted it.

"It's not good calling me names. If you don't go right now I'm going to call the police."

On my way out I passed an old woman in a white uniform. Her kyphosis was exaggerated by the concentration she gave to a corruption on the floor. She kept stirring this with a mop during our brief conversation.

"Did you work here eight years ago?" I asked.

"Yes."

"Do you remember a Mr. Peckham who was here then for a few days?"

"I don't know. That's too long ago."

"Is there a Mr. Peckham here now?" I asked.

"I don't know."

There was nothing more to do there, and I reached the door with a feeling of certainty that if I got away before the petulant call for Mildred came again, all would be well. Unfairly, it disregarded physical laws, and after I'd closed the door and reached the top of the ramp I heard it once more.

I ran and, gaining speed from the ramp, shot out into the street where the bargain that had been made was almost paid off. When I was just short of the opposite curb a car barely missed me and amid whirlpools of debris turned the corner at the end of the block. The driver had not only been going too fast, he had been on the wrong side of the street.

36

I WENT to my room in the residents' quarters, took off my clothes, and, as I stuffed them into a plastic bag, noticed that I had had a bright blue Conklin in my shirt pocket. After showering for twenty minutes I went to the phone and called Grace on the ward.

"I won't be home tonight."

"Why not? You're not on call."

"I have to follow a twenty-four-hour routine of fasting, showering, and abstinence in order to purify myself so I can come back to you."

"Stephen, what is the matter with you?"

"Miasmic marasmus. I have been steeped with malignant humors."

"What? What are you talking about? Where are you?"

"I'm in the residents' quarters—I'm not fit for human cohabitation. If you touch me now you may turn gray and pulpy. But I'll see you tomorrow; then I'll be decontaminated."

"Stephen, you don't make sense. What's happened to you?"

"Putrescine and cadavarine have replaced some of my essential amino acids, including those of my bone marrow."

"Stephen, I'm coming over."

"No, you can't do that. Please don't come; I know how to manage this."

But she had hung up. I was back in the shower again when there was a knocking at the door and I heard her call me.

I went to the door and shouted, "Grace, please go away. I

promise I'll be there tomorrow night. I'm all right. I know what I'm doing."

"Open the door."

"No, you can't come in."

"Is someone else in there?"

"No."

"Open the door or I'll get the janitor."

I opened the door.

She came in and I retreated across the room.

"See, there's no one here. Now go home and shower. Don't stay any longer."

"Stephen, where are your clothes? What's in that bag?"

"My clothes."

"Tell me what's happened."

I told her a little bit about the lizard's place.

"Are you going to burn your clothes?"

"Yes."

"Your shoes too?"

"Especially my shoes."

"That's silly. Here," and she started for the bag, but I grabbed it and held it behind me.

"Stephen, give that to me. I'll get them cleaned."

"You don't know what you're saying. You don't know what you are dealing with. These clothes can't be worn again. They may have already rotted."

"Give me the bag."

"Stay away; if you don't go I'll run out of the room."

"With no clothes?"

"Yes." I started for the door.

"Let's sit down and talk."

"O.K., you sit over there."

"Is your suit in there?"

"It *was* my suit. Excuse me," I said, and I got a pair of shorts from my drawer and slipped them on.

"How about your billfold? Your cards and identification? Is your billfold in the bag?"

"Yes."

"And your fountain pen?"

"Yes."

"It must have really been horrible."

"Yes; now will you go?"

"What are you going to do?"

"Fast, shower, take a Fleets enema and a purgative. I won't go to the ward tomorrow, but I'll see you again tomorrow night. Weak but pure."

"I can make you weak, and who wants to be pure?"

"This isn't funny."

"Show me what's in the bag."

"No."

"I'll sit over here clear across the room. Then I'll go."

I took the bag to the farthest corner and looked in. My suit was still there. It was wrinkled but didn't even smell.

"It's my suit," I said.

"Hold it up."

I did. Aside from the wrinkles it was no different than when I'd put it on that morning.

"What else is in there?"

I took out my shirt, underwear, and shoes. None of the rest of my clothes had suffered any more than the suit.

Her presence had purified the lot. There was no odor, no slime, nothing but my wrinkled clothes.

"Put them back in the bag and I'll have them cleaned."

"I think you're just wonderful," I said.

"It's nothing; we go by a cleaners every day."

"Maybe the suit only needs pressing," I said, and handed her the bag.

37

ONE HUNDRED SIXTY-EIGHT HOURS AND THIRTY-TWO—I mean, a few days after my trip to Merri Hours—Mrs. Vukov called me. She talked rapidly, barely pausing now and then for a breath.

"I guess you really are a doctor if you work at the hospital and they think you're a doctor. I read about a man who pretended to be a doctor and everyone thought he was, but he wasn't, but it isn't likely that you're pretending to be a doctor. I asked for Dr. Boyd when they said this was the hospital and you called back, so you're a doctor. Not that everybody at the hospital is a doctor, for there are nurses and orderlies and internes and clerks and patients and then there is Ernest who, as they say, is something else. And Ernest is what you wanted to talk about. That makes you a special doctor, for of all the doctors that Ernest has had you are the only one that thought that Ernest was something else. When I said, 'as they say, Ernest is something else' I didn't mean anyone is saying Ernest is something else 'cause they aren't. For a long time he's been careful that no one knows he's something else. Ernest does not like attention, but he is what you wanted to talk about and I can talk now 'cause I've gotten away. I shouldn't say I've gotten away when I just walked out of my own house. That's not getting away to just walk out of your own house. If that's getting away then everybody's getting away every day because nearly everybody walks out of their own house every day unless of course they're sick and lying in bed and even then they might get worse and have to go to the hospital in an ambulance so you can't say that those in bed never leave the house.

"But I can talk now 'cause I've gotten away and there's nobody listening in. Of course you can't say 'nobody,' for there is Ernest, who is always listening. Did you know he was listening, dear Dr. Boyd?"

"Yes," I said without thinking.

"He's listening but he doesn't count because he doesn't care. Did you know he didn't care, dear Dr. Boyd?"

"No."

"When I said he didn't count I didn't mean, one, two, three, because he could do that before he was born; I mean when he truly doesn't care at all it makes no difference whether he listens or not. Isn't that right, Ernest?"

She paused. "See, he doesn't bother to answer. And Mrs. Prine isn't listening: She's lying on the floor with blood in her hair."

"What happened to Mrs. Prine?"

"A vase dropped on her head; it's badly broken—not her head, it's badly bleeding."

"Is she alone?"

"Is she alone? She says she's never alone, that God is with her always, but she was alone when I left. I don't know if she is alone now."

I asked for her number and told her I would call her back. Then I phoned the police and gave them the address where I thought there was an unconscious woman on the floor.

She began talking as soon as she was back on the line.

"You called somebody about Mrs. Prine. Well, you're a doctor and you know best. If you think she shouldn't lie on the floor you know best. Even I know she shouldn't lie on the floor. It's just that I played a game after I left that I used to play with Ernest, the 'Let It Not Be' game. It always worked then, but that was a long time ago."

"Where are you? I'll come and we will talk about Ernest."

"Meet me on the farm. It's where I always go when I get away. I'll be swinging while I wait." And abruptly she hung up.

Meet me on the farm, she had said, but what farm? Wherever it was, she wouldn't be free very long, for it was a place she had gone to before. Perhaps someone was already waiting there to take her back. But if they weren't and I got there first I'd learn among

147

other things about the "Let It Not Be" game. The implication in the name of their childhood pastime appalled me.

It wasn't until Grace and I were driving home that I guessed what Mrs. Vukov had meant.

I didn't mention the name that had become an anathema to Grace but asked that we drive through the park where we had picnicked once.

The road curved around clumps of ancient evergreen trees the homesteaders had left and through lawns that had been fields. We heard the laughing, shouting children in the wading pool before we came to the playground on our right.

The empty slide reflected the afternoon sun in my eyes, blinding me momentarily. Then I saw that among the creaking, pumping swings there was one that was still. On it sat a gray-haired child wearing a long mink coat.

"Let's stop a minute," I said. "There is someone there I have to see."

"Christ, I should have known," Grace said, but she parked the car.

We got out and she followed me across the grass to the dust around the swings.

She was a tiny woman with a face that was narrow at the sides and plump in front so that her cheeks kept her eyes from opening wide. Her skin was surprisingly brown for a person who had spent much time in confinement.

"You're beautiful," she said to Grace. "When I saw you coming I thought there is a girl who might be a movie star playing a nurse. But it's not likely you're a movie star because there aren't any cameras, so you are a nurse. Would you like to swing?"

"No, thank you," Grace said.

"Would you like to wear my coat? It may be too warm, but it is wonderful protection."

"No, thank you," Grace said again.

I introduced ourselves and led Mrs. Vukov to where a picnic table was shaded by trees.

"When did I know Ernest was different?" She repeated my

question. "I knew it yesterday and the day before that and last week and last year—"

"When did you first know Ernest was different?"

"It wasn't when the questions started before mother went to the hospital. Over and over, 'Who are you? Who am I?' I thought all babies that were coming did that even when Mother and Father laughed and said it was imagination. And it wasn't when the questions became 'Who are they?' and 'Why are they different from you?' and Mother and Father never really laughed again.

"It wasn't the time after Mommy went to the hospital when the anger came in the night like a flashcracker going off in my head.

"It was when they started asking questions about Ernest that I knew he was different. If grownups got upset it had to be unusual for babies to pick at minds."

"Tell me about the games you played."

"Well, there was the 'Let It Not Be' game and the 'Change the Clock' game and the 'Ride the Furniture' game. That's all part of the things we keep in a trunk in storage.

"You have to call at least twice to get them to bring it in a truck and then you have to have them leave it somewhere out of the way and you may not even notice it there and when you do you're likely to call and have them take it back again. But if not, you have to find the key, and that can take days, and even then you might lose it again for days at a time. But here we are: I have the key; if you're ready we'll look in.

"Here we have the 'Change the Clock' game. It's wonderful for playing on the way to school and still not be late and you can put off your homework as long as you want and still finish it in time for bed, and if you have to recite in front of the class it's over in seconds and you're in your seat again. Lovely, lovely.

"And here we have the 'Let It Not Be' game. Nothing broken that can't be fixed, just like new. You can eat your ice cream cone over and over and never get full. You can fall in a puddle and walk around it again as clean as you please.

"And the 'Ride the Furniture' game: swooping about the house on a hassock, but you must be sure the curtains are pulled.

"Now I guess we can close the trunk and lose the key and send it back to storage again."

"How about that compartment?"

"Oh, you noticed. I'd rather not look there if you please. There's really no point. It takes another key, and it's lost."

"Send it back to storage," Grace said. "We've seen enough."

"No, no," I said. "I want you to open that compartment."

"Well, you're a doctor and you know best; it's been a long time, but here we are again. Terrible. Terrible. The same games but all wrong. Everything's backward. Now forever in front of the class the words come so slow. The good things go so fast they're a blur, so you're dizzy and nothing's good now. You try to fix something and you break more things but you can't keep from trying even though you know what'll happen. Through the house the hassock's chasing you now. It's all wrong, wrong, wrong. Mother says she'll take my place and Ernest is mad 'cause she's wrecked the experiment and gives her a migraine and I try to stay in the closet."

She sat across from us, her knees pulled up to her chin and her eyes closed.

"Oh, that dirty son-of-a-bitch," Grace's voice quavered.

"Is there one more compartment?"

"Shut up," Grace said. "You're as bad as him."

Mrs. Vukov opened her eyes. "You're nice but you should have worn the coat; Adrian doesn't like them to shoot through this coat."

I turned on the bench and looked behind us. Beside a large tree twenty-six feet from our table the insurance adjuster who had relaxed on our couch kneeled by his open briefcase. He looked up, caught my eye, and brought out one hand from behind the lid to wave to me. A moment later he raised a rifle and fired.

38

THE FIRST SHOT hit Grace. Laterally where her right hip began the curve to her waist a three-inch syringe made a dimple in her uniform. She stood up and was unaware of what had happened until I pulled it out. With my arm around her I tried to help her over the bench, but her foot caught. As we fell I heard the rifle fire again.

Whatever had been in the syringe had no apparent effect, for she was up as soon as I. Hand in hand we ran for the nearest tree.

There were no more shots. The only sound was the distant laughing and yelling from the pool. I looked out and saw that the man had broken down his gun and was packing it back in the case.

"I think I'll sit down for a minute," Grace said.

"No, let's try to get to the car." I put my arms around her but the noise from the children faded and I almost fell. Then I found the syringe that was sticking in my left shoulder. I put it in my pocket and we started. In the first ten yards I knew we would never make it, and a little farther Grace stumbled and we fell.

I concentrated on standing and heard someone say, "How about a hand?"

"Thanks a lot," I said, and remember feeling grateful, for Grace was sprawled on the ground and I knew I could never get her up by myself.

"Thanks a lot," I said but, oddly, this time it was for being helped out of a car.

We were in a large parking garage with fluorescent lights

151

overhead. Both of the men who had been in the apartment were there, but I didn't see Mrs. Vukov.

They were well prepared. We were put in wheelchairs and wheeled into an elevator. The heavy feeling from the acceleration and the opposite when we stopped made me nauseated. Grace stirred and tried to get out of her chair but the man who had guarded the door pushed her back.

We went by a door marked "A. Vukov and Associates" to another one with the word "Private" on it, and here they tapped on the pane.

The door opened and we were pushed into a large office. A plump man in an iridescent suit walked away from us then turned and faced us from behind a flat-topped desk. He had graying reddish hair, heavy sideburns, sharp features, and a red face. His voice shook when he spoke.

"I'll call you Mr. Boyd. Believe me, you're finished as a doctor."

"I hold you responsible for what happened to my wife's nurse, you fool. You had to meddle in what didn't concern you."

Grace spoke; her voice was normal.

"You people will just get into more trouble if you don't let us leave right now."

"Shut up," he said, and turned back to me. "The best that can be said for you is that you're incompetent, but I'm inclined to think you're crazy. You have got my wife stirred up over some quack remedy you've been trying on her brother. Don't you understand we've had real doctors—good doctors with experience—who have given up on him?"

So this was the vehicle, I thought, that carried Mr. Peckham to safety years ago.

What had that been like? Did he remember? Had he even been aware of where he was, or had he acted automatically without consciousness or memory?

"Why did you bring us here?" Grace said.

"I want a sensible answer as to what's going on at that hospital with my brother-in-law. Furthermore, I mean to put a stop to it once and for all." He was blustering. His assurance was gone.

"You do remember," I said. "Plainer than yesterday."

Not surprisingly, the effect of their tranquilizer was similar to that of alcohol. As I had at the party I was able to concentrate on many things at once, Then it had been the various conversations around me, but now there was an important difference.

There was the furious red-faced man who was neither furious nor red-faced now.

There was a room thick with smoke. Here and there furniture loomed, dimly lit by the flicker of a burning curtain. And all about there was the incessant crackling like hundreds of strings of firecrackers and the fierce heat.

And finally there was the scarred, scrabbling, amorphous thing that struggled to get free.

Mr. Vukov leaned on the desk. His mouth was open, and without moving his lips he began repeating a sound like uhhh-huh with the uhhh drawn out and ending in a squeak and a short huh.

The fierce heat on my hands and face and where my clothes touch when my legs move. It was their plan, not mine. They were the ones that were willing to die. If I could breathe, or if I'm not to breathe, if I could drown in a clear, cold pool. Down I'm going, not falling but kneeling, and now that—that thing's on my back.

He must have lost consciousness then, for that scene ended and at the same time what I had held broke loose and scuttled away.

In his rumpled, iridescent suit Mr. Vukov looked like a maimed bird as he hopped over to the window and then up on the sill. The glass cracked in a star-shaped pattern and he fell back inside.

He landed on his feet and went careening along the walls clear around the room. He picked up speed all the way as though learning to use his legs again. On his second try at the window he didn't even touch the sill.

153

39

GLASS was still falling from the window when Grace and I left the room. I saw by the light above the elevator that we were on the twenty-fourth floor.

Down on the street, we walked away from the crowd that was forming until we found a cab. When we were inside Grace moved to a corner and sat staring ahead with her hands clenched in her lap.

"It was a frightening afternoon," I said. "That is, while we were awake."

She didn't answer, but folded her arms tightly under her breasts and shivered.

I wondered what must she think of the strange goings-on that had started with a ride in the park.

Why would that man want two strangers there to witness his suicide? And then he ran around the room knocking over furniture like a blind person trying to get away. How horrible, that sound he made.

Her shaking became worse, and I remembered the devastating effect my curiosity had had on Mr. Vukov and deliberately tried to turn my mind to other things.

There was enough to think about, for the abnormal intensification of recollection was the same after the tranquilizer as it had been with alcohol. I began by going over the references to telepathy that had appeared in all the journals I'd seen, but still her thoughts intruded.

He must have had some sort of seizure. There is a name for that, but I can't remember it.

"A psychomotor equivalent seizure," I said, and was about to give her a description straight from a neurology text when I realized she hadn't asked aloud.

"I thought he might have had that, too," she said, "but I couldn't remember the name."

"It's possible," I said, and now I was free to quote from the pages. But it was a dull description for her to follow, and soon her mind began to wander.

It sounds as though he were reading that. It's that strange mind of his. What did he say when we got in the cab? He made some joke!

I shouted, "Whoa; I know what we forgot: the car. Driver, take us to the park."

I had to distract her several times to keep from being made uncomfortable by her thinking. Once after we had been to the park, I even asked her to stop the car and got out and pretended to retch as though I were sick.

As soon as we were back in the apartment, she got out the phone book.

"Who are you going to call?" I asked.

"I'm going to call the police and see if I can make them believe that while I was sitting in the park some nut shot me in the butt with a blowgun. Then I'm going to call the hospital and tell them I won't be to work tomorrow."

That I had not anticipated her second remark relieved me, for it meant that my freakish power was diminishing and I could concentrate on the argument that was coming without having to sort out words from thoughts.

"Let's talk it over first," I said.

"What is there to talk over? We were kidnaped; I think that makes it an FBI case."

"I know that and that's partly why I don't know if we should report it; I hate to get them mixed up in this."

"Mixed up in what? Why should you hate to have them mixed up in anything?"

"Well, Dr. Hahn wouldn't like the notoriety for the hospital.

It would be in the papers, our living arrangement here would become common knowledge; after all, nobody was hurt."

"Somebody was hurt. A man jumped out of a window. And whether I was hurt or not, I don't particularly care to have my ass made a dartboard, and as far as that goes, I wouldn't think you would either. Not calling the police is the craziest thing I ever heard of. If we don't, those men may be back, and playing watchdog might not work next time."

"They won't be back; they weren't the ones who were interested in Mr. Peckham."

"There's a lot about that vegetable I don't understand. I'm not saying I won't call the police, but if you don't tell me everything about him I'll call them for sure, and I'm through arguing."

"O.K." There was no help for it. She had meant what she said.

I didn't leave out anything. She stopped me once when I was telling about the swan and then said, "Oh, go ahead, what I'd say wouldn't make any difference anyway."

I finished by telling her about reading her mind on the way home.

"I would have told you this a long time ago but you wouldn't have believed it then any more than you do now. I didn't think Mr. Peckham wanted it known either, but better you than the FBI."

She had gotten up and walked around at times while I talked, and that was what she was doing when I came to the end. Her face was white, and she wouldn't look at me directly.

"All right," she said, "I won't call the police if you'll promise two things."

I waited for the conditions and finally had to ask, "What are they?"

"That you see a psychiatrist and that you don't go back to the hospital any more."

"But my work at the hospital is better than it ever was."

"That's not the point. You're not going to get well until you're away from there."

"I'm not sure I'm sick."

156

"Of course you are. Those words come from your head, the same place all that strange information comes from, only it's real and the words aren't. I'm not going to try to make you believe it because I know I can't, but if you don't get treatment and give up your residency I'll call the police and the FBI and tell them all about this afternoon. And what's more, I'll tell them everything you told me about your friend in the trance. If you don't want the whistle blown on him, you'll do as I say."

"Aren't you afraid that if I'm thwarted I'll become violent?"

"Don't be silly."

The bargain we finally made was that I would see the psychiatrist and follow his advice as to whether or not I continued working.

We sent out for pizza then and while we were waiting for it and while we ate it there was no mention of my delusions.

We had been in bed eighty-three minutes (oddly, the ratio of her orgasms to mine at 5.33 was nearly half again the usual) when she asked,

"Now how could you think that vegetable could have anything to do with us?"

I mumbled as though I were falling asleep. How, I wondered, can she believe I'm managing on my own?

Before I did go to sleep, I tried to visualize my third-grade primer and found I could. The abnormal facility of recall had never lasted so long.

40

WE SPENT part of our lunch hour the next day at a phone booth down by the main entrance to the hospital. Grace had gotten from somewhere the names of four psychiatrists, but none of their secretaries would give us an appointment sooner than a month. I tried to look properly disappointed, but this is what I'd counted on when I'd made the bargain. When Grace took over the phone and said it was an emergency she was told that I should go directly into the hospital and the doctor would see me at once. While we argued, visitors on their way into the hospital turned to look at Grace who, they must have thought, was prettier than and as upset as any nurse on afternoon TV.

"It won't be so bad," she said. "I'll come and see you every day and stay as long as they will let me."

"No. Remember our bargain. The first rule of psychotherapy is never go back on your word to a nut. The hospital is a place for people who are dangerous to themselves or others or who can't function outside it. I'm not dangerous to anyone, and I've never functioned better."

"If you believe," she said, "what you told me, you made that man jump out the window."

"That was a harmless delusion; he was despondent over his wife's illness like the morning paper said."

"At least quit working here," she said. "This place isn't good for you."

"We'll try it a little longer," I said, "and see how it goes. Anyway, they are counting on me to present a case at the staff conference."

We were still arguing when we went up to lunch. It would come up again, of course, but for the moment I had gotten by without even making an appointment.

The meaning of the communication I received the next morning was unmistakable, and I acted promptly.

That afternoon while we were driving home I began.

"Grace, you're not only sure I'm sick, but you are sure I'll get well, eventually, aren't you?"

"Oh, yes," she said. "The important thing is to get away from that hospital and get some treatment." She may have thought that at last I was ready to listen to reason.

"What I'm leading up to," I said, "is a proposal of marriage. I know you think I'm psychotic, but if you're sure I'll get well like you say, that shouldn't make too much difference. We have never talked about it, but I've thought about it enough. We know each other pretty well; I guess you know me better than anyone, and I know I'll never find—"

She interrupted, "I'll marry you if that's what you want."

"We'll leave the hospital at noon tomorrow and we'll get married in three days," I said.

"My parents will be pleased. They haven't been too happy with our arrangement."

"Will your father be pleased?" I asked.

She laughed. "It will be all right; you didn't either one see each other at your best."

Two blocks farther, she pulled over and parked the car.

"Stephen, tell me the truth. Did Mr. Peckham have anything to do with this?"

"Yes, he did."

"What was it?"

"This morning, 'Altar ten'; I don't see how it could mean anything else."

She sat looking ahead, her hands still on the wheel. "Stephen, Stephen, Stephen," she said, "don't you see? Now we can't. It's the one thing that could stop it, and now we can't."

"I don't see why not," I said.

"It would just make you worse. We have got to show you that those words don't mean anything at all. Now I don't know when I can marry you, if ever," and she started to cry. Then she said, "You drive the rest of the way."

"I don't know how."

"Well learn, for Christ's sake, learn. Maybe if you could do more things like a normal person, you wouldn't be such a nut." Then she cried harder and said between sobs, "I'm sorry, I didn't mean that."

"I know I'm going to have to learn to drive. I'm going to take lessons, but I've been so busy with this Peckham business—"

"Peckham, Peckham, screw Peckham! That living corpse is

159

dominating your life. Don't you see that? And mine, too, now. Give me some Kleenex. If you'd only asked me before he said it."

"Aw, come on now," and suddenly the roles were reversed. "Come on now," I said. "You know the word came from my mind even if I attribute it to Mr. Peckham. You're beginning to sound like me."

"That's right, but it was just a slip. What I mean is if you had just thought of it some other way, but now we just can't. You may follow those damned directions, but I never will."

"If you won't because he said it you're letting him dominate your life more than I am."

"Stop it; you're mixing me up. He's not dominating anything, me or anyone else, it's just this delusion you have that's causing our trouble, and if we marry now it's reinforced."

She started the car.

I said, "I have some arguments; you listen and don't interrupt and see if when I'm done you don't agree. I'll wait till we get home; then you'll be able to pay attention to them."

"Oh, tell me now; driving is not all that complicated: I can listen and drive."

"O.K. First, we would like to get married. Second, I did think of it long ago, but this has always seemed like a poor time."

"What makes it better right now? Just because you got a communication on your hot line to the vegetable kingdom."

"Now wait a minute—you said you'd listen."

"I'm sorry, I'll be quiet."

I leaned over and kissed her.

"I can drive and listen but I can't drive if you start that. I can't do much of anything if you start that. That's not fair."

It was true, and through all our problems I'd known that whether it was Mr. Peckham or not, when it came right down to it, I could have made her agree to anything, promise anything, do anything, for with a little persuasive talk and some sex play she was helpless. It was a weapon I hoped I didn't have to use because it seemed like a betrayal and not made any better by the knowledge that she could have done the same thing to me.

"Well, I've wanted to all along, I'd have given my right arm at the elbow at least before you knew I existed. Now, third: For the purposes of this discussion, I'll agree that the word 'altar' came from me. Fourth, if we let that stop us we are letting, we will say now, my delusions affect our activities more than if we went ahead. Fifth, I have no living relatives—none. Sixth, you think I'm psychotic, and even I am uncertain at times and especially the past two days, since I've been talking about it to you."

She started to say something but I held up a hand. "Please, I know you're sorry and it's for my own good; anyhow, for the purposes of this discussion, six, we think I'm nuts. Seven: When a person is nuts and may go into an acute psychotic episode at any moment, which I won't, but again for the purposes of this discussion we will say I might, who commits him? Answer: the nearest relative. Who now commits me if it happened here?" We were home and sitting in the car in front of the apartment. "If it happened here and now, a complicated thing—no relatives; it has to be done by the courts, a guardian has to be appointed, probably some lawyer appointed by a judge." I was excited because I saw now I could easily get to ten. "Eight, you marry me, who commits me? You do. At a moment's notice, at the first bubbly froth on my lips, at the first rant, long before the raves, and whisk! I'm off to the hatch for the boobies. Nine, if it doesn't work out, so what? A single Grace Boyd is better than a single Grace Waggoner. You'll save time when you write checks, for one thing. And ten, last and most, I love you devotedly, passionately, foreveredly, you are the ultimate, the epitome of all that makes women dear to men."

"All right," Grace said, "I'm convinced. We will get married. Tomorrow we'll get the license. Now let's go to the grocery store. We'll get some steaks and wine. This calls for another celebration."

"Great," I said, "but I'll take sparkling grape juice. I'm still on the wagon."

41

EARLY SATURDAY afternoon we drove to the Hinney house, where the ceremony was to be. Again I had the feeling that the area was familiar to me and that momentarily I would remember all the details of being there before, and again the feeling left me when we went into the house.

Mr. Hinney repeated jokes he had probably heard at his own wedding about being nervous and that there was still time to back out. What made me nervous was what I saw on the dining room table. There in an ice bucket were two bottles of champagne.

Sue Hinney asked Grace if she wasn't worried about seductive female patients. "I read about them in a magazine. Tell me, how do you handle them?" she asked me.

"Did you say 'how,' or 'how many'?" Richard asked.

"Let him answer," Sue said.

"I don't remember ever having had one," I said, and I didn't.

"The fools," Grace said.

"This article said it was a real problem," Sue said. "Maybe you don't recognize them."

"The ones that won't put their clothes on when the examination is over are the seductive ones," Richard said.

"One of my clinical professors in medical school," I said, "he was little, almost a dwarf, and very ugly, said that he frequently had the problem. He told them they had a distinctive odor that was unpleasant to him. He claimed that invariably worked."

"That would do for me." Sue said.

A justice of the peace, who someone other than I had remembered to call, arrived, and a few minutes later we were married.

There were kisses and congratulations and then a pop and a cork ricocheted about the room.

The toasts began, and of course with those came the syndrome of complete recall. I expected it and planned to do as I had done at Dr. Adler's, simply reject, before making, all comments for which there weren't numerous and recent sources. What I wasn't prepared for was an awareness of what everyone in the room was thinking.

How many brides, I wonder, wake up on their wedding day on top of the groom? Stephen looks flustered. He imagines, I suppose, that the champagne is making him remember everything. Why won't he accept the simple fact of his brilliance?

Lucky little stick. Jesus, I wonder if she's as good a piece of ass as she looks. But I'll never know; I'm too normal.

This is the second time I've been to a Grace's wedding. I don't know, he's not another Gerry, but there is something strange about him. Why does she—

"A toast," I shouted, and jumped to my feet, "a toast to our good friends with this spinoff product of the corks invention." Only momentarily was I rid of them.

We'd better leave, I've seen this before—he just gets worse.

Jesus, does he ever have a burr up his ass all of a sudden.

The only woman who would try and seduce him would be another freak collector. Poor Grace, where does she find them?

"Excuse me." Wine slopped from the glass that I almost dropped on the table, and I bolted from the room. Locked away in their bathroom, I began the process of learning to keep minds out.

The answer I found was concentration. Where the reflection from the window softened the surface of the almost spherical brass doorknob, I made an entry and left them all behind. Thirteen minutes later Grace knocked on the door and said it was time to go.

When I came out they were waiting, but I kept ahead most of the time. From the doorknob to a bar of a towel rack and then into my watch. When I couldn't stand the crashing wheels any longer I shouted "Ho" and made it almost untouched into the unopened bottle of champagne. I hadn't reckoned with the pressure, and just before I lost consciousness I tried for a prism on the chandelier. A mistake, it offered no protection at all, and worse, I bounded about inside it, a prisoner. With another "Ho" I jumped straight up and landed flat-footed. It worked. I got into my head that was reflected in the mirror above the buffet. I was alone there.

"Grace, you can't possibly take him anywhere when he's like that. I'll call a doctor."

"Now that," I said, "is carrying coals to Newcastle, population 1901 215,328." But I was rapidly getting my bearings.

"You're all right?" Grace had led me from the bathroom but had backed away from me at my first "Ho."

"Never better. I apologize for the display. I had," I lied, "a hypoglycemic episode brought on by the wine, which though excellent I thought a trifle sweet."

Before we left I gave Mr. Hinney ten dollars, explaining that it was a superstition of mine that I contribute to the cost of my wedding. He took it without arguing.

Outside, as though a lens had been twisted to focus, the feeling of familiarity was memory. I knew exactly when I'd been there before.

42

ONCE, suspended over the sidewalk, I had traveled by here almost daily. Sometimes I had held the bar of colored beads with both hands and, leaning far back, had looked up onto the layers of leaves, and where these were thinner had tried to match the squeak of the wheel to the patches of light above. Two blocks down on this side of the street we would turn onto the front walk of a big brown house with white pillars. After bumping me backward up the steps my mother would lift me from the stroller and carry me up to a housekeeping room on the second floor. I had lived there with her in what, if it was not complete happiness, was almost unvarying contentment. But everything had changed when the shouting man came.

In the precise after-image characteristic of my syndrome I saw him far more clearly now than I had as a child, for then I had been fascinated with the soft glow of his boots and the brass buttons far above on a level with my mother.

I recognized him with the shock one feels on seeing an acquaintance unthought of for years. The man was younger, browner, and thinner than I remembered, but he was unmistakably my father.

I'd finally dared to crawl toward those boots when somehow I knew that because of me their voices had stopped. I started to cry, and when my mother picked me up his shouting began. We still heard him on the stairs after he had slammed the door.

He came back every two or three days. As in a time-sequence film, spots appeared on the jacket with the sergeant's stripes, scuffs came on the boots, the trousers grew baggy, and one day his tie was permanently gone.

The loud voice that had frightened me then I understood now. There was much repetition, but the content of the outbursts gradually changed as the uniform got shabbier. The curses became demands, first for explanations, then for assurances of better conduct and finally, more than a month after the visits started, that she take him back.

My mother, who till then had answered in monosyllables when she answered at all, gave him her terms: There would be no explanations or assurances and no more requests for these; if he came back he was to do his best to be my father; if he couldn't accept this he was not to visit us again.

He was back four days later dressed as a civilian, and not long after that, our family left the apartment and the city.

The pattern in the threadbare carpet, the dust shining in the sunlight that came through a tear in the plastic curtain, the name she had assumed on her mailbox on the proch were details that were being added, but by the time we got in Grace's car the essentials of the recollection were complete.

"How do you feel now?" Grace was behind the wheel but she hadn't started the car. "Are you all right?"

"Yes."

"You've never acted like that before. Do you think we should call one of those doctors and put you in a hospital?"

"No, but before we go to the beach (we had planned a three-day stay at a motel on an ocean beach) I want to go out to Harbor Hospital. I'll show you the way. There is something there, a record of a patient, I have to see."

I'd expected she might argue, but she didn't even ask who the patient was.

"All right." She started the car. "There is a law against one-arm drivers, but one-arm passengers are O.K."

I knew now why the street had seemed changed. The trees and shrubbery had grown.

43

I suppose he is a doctor or else he would never have come back again, but it takes forever to find anything down there.

"I'll be glad to look through them myself," I said.

Mrs. Kappleman was startled, for I had for the first time intentionally "read a mind."

I don't want him or anyone else for that matter to see what a mess those files are in.

Bare electric globes lit twelve-by-twelve timbers that went up to the joists above; along a cement wall were stacked cardboard and wooden boxes filled with manila folders.

It's not once in ten years anyone asks for a chart that old. I don't think we have to keep them for more than five years. I'll pretend they aren't even there.

"I've more or less left the care of the records to the record librarian, who won't be back till Monday." *Why should I have a record librarian to find one chart every ten years?* "I believe charts that old may have been destroyed. State law only requires us to keep them five years."

But I had the advantage of knowing when she was lying.

"As your record librarian knows, state law requires that you keep them indefinitely. I understand that you're short of help and they are not in order."

I tried something else then for the first time. I looked directly at her and concentrated on projecting each word.

I want to see those files, now.

I wasn't prepared for the effect on her.

"Of course," she said, and slumped in her chair.

Did he do that? He can stay there as long as he wants. I don't care, if he doesn't do that anymore. Maybe I'm having a stroke. Something happened, but it couldn't have been him, could it?

"How do we get to the basement?" I asked.

"By the nurses' station there's a door on the left; I'd show you but I'm afraid I'm not well."

Does he know I'm not well? Did he do that?

I found what I was looking for in the eighteenth box counting from the corner. Mr. Peckham's chart here was much the same as his chart at the hospital. I hadn't expected otherwise.

What I also expected and what I found was that some of the nurses' notes were in my mother's familiar handwriting and bore her signature.

44

LATE THE NEXT MORNING the sound of the turf woke me. An arthropod—class, Insecta; subclass, Pterygota; division, Holometabola; order, Diptera; suborder, Cyclorrhapha; tribe, Schizophora; genus and species, *Musca domestica*—described an $r^2=a^2\theta$ curve before landing on a coffee cup smudged with lipstick.

I closed my eyes and tried to go back to sleep, but my mind was busy sketching some episodes from my past and minutely detailing others. The bizarre syndrome had lasted all night. I suspected then that it might be permanent, and so far it has been.

The man I had thought was my father had tried to keep the bargain, but hostility is all the more threatening by usually being elaborately concealed. His real antagonism had been revealed to me on a subconscious level by the grating that sometimes came in his voice, the quick narrowing of his eyes, and the often too-firm grip on my shoulder. As a result, instead of a normal and transient fear of castration, mine was a persistent dread, and my frantic gathering of fountain pens was a dynamic mechanism designed to perplex my enemy with an inexhaustible supply of appendages.

Had my mother even known (any more than Mrs. Bailey had known when she canceled the ambulance that would have taken Mr. Peckham back to the nursing home) of the incident that had resulted in my life? If she were aware and thought she was acting because of some overwhelming and perverse need in herself, wouldn't she have done something to interrupt or prevent the pregnancy? The notes on the chart I had seen gave no clue. But could I expect "The young man in Room 18 was very restless tonight and was not quieted until I had been in his bed a half hour"?

It was possible that Mr. Peckham had left a posthypnotic suggestion that prevented her from considering an abortion. His sister thought him unconcerned with events about him, but might I not have been an exception?

And why had I chosen that particular residency when I could have gotten better ones? If I had applied for it, I might have obtained on my own the position Dr. Adler had offered me, but I had thought that a state hospital would offer a wider variety of cases. Well, I'd been right on that score. But had I acted voluntarily? There were other state hospitals I could have gone to, and that I had chosen the one where my real father was a patient seemed much more likely to have been arranged than a coincidence.

One thing was certain: I could not let Grace (her leg, limp and slightly moist from the overly warm bed, was across me) go back to work at the hospital.

Last night when the manager had turned on the light and stepped aside and I'd followed her into this cabin she had been as pleased as I'd ever seen her. I started a fire in the big stone fireplace that took up most of one wall and we lay on a blanket and watched the flames.

"Let's not go back," she had said. "We can call up and resign our jobs. We can stay here six weeks, and by then you'll be well. Then you can look for a residency in something else, maybe dermatology. We'll start a family, and every summer we'll come here for a month."

"They are counting on me to present a case at the next staff conference."

"So what if they are? They can get someone else. Anyway, you can't tell them all the things you believe about that mushroom."

"That's exactly what I'm going to do," I said.

"What? You can't, not in front of all those people. You'll no more than get started and they'll have you in a private room yourself."

"Well, that's what you wanted, that I go into a hospital, and telling my story to forty psychiatrists should be at least as good as telling it to one."

"It's not the same."

"No," I said, "but if I present him exactly the way I would any other case and like I've been trained to do, giving all the laboratory work, my observations, and my conclusions, then it seems to me I'm making the most sane response I could to the whole business. And if I do anything else I'll never know whether I acted on my own or not, and more and more I'm wondering how much he controls people without them ever even remembering what they have done."

"Stephen, Stephen," she had said. "Well then, after the staff conference what do you think about dermatology?"

"Why particularly that?"

"Oh, I don't know. I wouldn't think there would be any tension, for one thing. And those seductive patients Sue was talking about, they couldn't look very good to you if they had a rash."

As usually happened when I thought of her, distension began in my corpora cavernosa. When I tried to slide from what had become the uncomfortable weight of her leg, it flexed and held me.

"If you remember everything," she said, "surely you know nobody with an erection gets out of a bed I'm in."

45

WHEN MRS. BAILEY had recommended the place, she had called it a motel, and I'd expected a brick-and-glass box crowded with others like it and set up high to improve the view and to provide a place for parked cars underneath, but it wasn't like that at all. Ours was one of a dozen gray shake cabins scattered among picturesquely twisted evergreen trees a few feet above the beach.

Here on the windward edge of forests that had stretched for a third of a continent the timber was too deformed for harvesting, but beginning a hundred yards inland it had all been logged off. Where the hills behind us formed the features of a dead giant there were stumps like whiskers grown out again before the funeral.

Just to the north, a ridge of land extended into the ocean as huge rocks. Most of the time these kept vehicles off of the beach in front of us, but when the tide was out they could get by. Each day the first to come were the motorcyclists, who, two to a machine, would time their dash to a period between waves—like I've heard the Mexican divers do. They were wild at first and raced up and down and cut figure eights in an elaborate mechanized courting ritual until the plain sightseers in campers and cars with license plates from all over the country could get through and by weight of numbers slow everything down. By the time the sun and the moon had begun to bring the water back and start the migration the other way, the motorcyclists had gone off somewhere, perhaps to reverse their position and copulate with the creatures who'd been clinging to them.

In spite of the traffic that crowded the beach, for a few hours every day we had a good time. We sat by driftwood fires at night under stars that were brighter than what we were used to in the city. We built sand castles, went beachcombing, and played in the surf. It was the sort of interlude that one would want to remember, but I became more and more concerned that I would remember too much.

How much expansion of consciousness could I tolerate? If I were forever to see the shape of each wave as it changed coming into the shore, then the pattern it made on the sand, and the water washing back to the next one, if it was to be the same for the footprints and tire tracks, some sharp and some drier and partly filled by the wind, and the turn in the grain of the driftwood and the folds in the polyethylene bags that here and there hung from it, the foliage higher up, and above that the whiskers even on the eyes of the figure on the hills, and the clouds that changed their form as I watched; if from now on I were permanently to record the whole hemisphere within my sight and hearing, wouldn't there be a limit? Wouldn't there be some point where my neurons would be so glutted and my association pathways so jammed with trivia that I could not accept any more? Would I then be a creature living in a past more vivid than anyone else's present but not even aware that I had become a vegetable, simply because I was unable to forget?

And what I was adding each moment did not compare in amount to what was coming to me in great swatches from my adolescence and beyond. Some of this material I had repressed, like how I had tried to comfort my mother after my father's death, but some I couldn't have known, for now I was able to read the titles of books my mother had checked out from the library when it had been the building with the pillars and I'd been less than three years old. My mind was becoming a photograph album in which I only appeared at the occasional times when I'd looked in a mirror—or more like an endless movie that could be stopped and each frame examined in detail. But it couldn't be endless; after all, I was only twenty-seven years old.

I decided that, until my past was more completely filled in, the common-sense thing to do was to limit my current impressions.

At a drugstore in a little resort village (it was here that the vehicles gained access to the beach), while Grace was shopping for groceries, I bought a pair of scissors, some black paper, some glue, and the darkest sunglasses I could find.

That afternoon I left Grace on the beach where she was watching some fishing boats with a pair of binoculars (I had avoided looking through these; after all, I was seeing too much as it was) and went back to our cabin. I got out the glasses, cut paper to fit, and glued it in place on the inside of the lenses.

After that when we sat on the driftwood to look at the ocean or lay in the sand or watched the fire at night and even when we walked, if I was sure there was an unobstructed beach ahead, I wore them.

This worked so well that I planned to get cotton for my ears on my next visit to the village, but Grace found me out.

"Let me try your glasses," she said, and before I could stop her had pulled them off my face and put them on.

"That's what I thought, you can't see anything," she said. Then she had them off and began picking at the paper.

"What have you done to these?"

"Don't," I said. "You'll ruin them." I saw the worried frown on her face before I blotted everything out again with the glasses.

I explained to her how, though I knew of no precedent, with a brain like a sponge that kept soaking things up but unlike a sponge could never be rung out, I was frightened at the prospect of saturation.

When I'd finished, she said, "Haven't you had patients who believed similar things?"

I hadn't, not that I could remember, but it was true some of them were convinced that odd conditions were affecting them. One man's delusion that he was melting down and running out the head of his penis as urine was as bizarre as any I'd come in contact with, but it had turned out that he'd been more right than any of the doctors he'd seen, for he had had a parathyroid tumor and his vertebrae were collapsing and the calcium had been going out in the urine.

"How do you think you can go back to work when you're like this?" she asked.

"Oh, I won't wear them at work. Just when I'm going back and forth so I won't remember every piece of waste paper I see and every brick in each building we pass, the cars, there are a thousand things I can cut out and never miss."

"Are you going to wear them to bed?"

"Of course not."

"Let's make reservations before we leave for a whole month here, right after the staff conference. If you tell them this like you've said you would, you'll be finished there. Perhaps you won't even last that long, because this effort to withdraw just means you're getting worse. But anyway, we'll spend a month here; you can wear your glasses and stuff cotton in your ears if you want to, but I think getting away from there will change everything."

We left the next morning. I didn't tell Grace, but that morning before we'd gotten up, another one of the messages had come. I'd decided to completely disregard all of them now. I knew Grace would be in favor of that and would think it was a sign I was better, but I was doing it only to make my data more complete and to see what happened when I wouldn't cooperate.

Grace asked the manager about reservations, but it turned out that we couldn't make them.

"None of this will be here by then," he said, and he seemed very enthusiastic, though what he told us must have meant that he was losing his job. "Bulldozers are coming in before then to level this whole place off. There's going to be a ninety-unit condominium go in here with an Olympic swimming pool, beauty shop, and restaurant. There will be parking for one and a half cars per unit and a gift shop. That's the coming thing now, condominiums, and this stretch of coast is about the prettiest anywhere. It's been overlooked for a long time, but not any more. Things are moving now."

46

ON OUR WAY BACK to the city I sat behind my dark glasses and tried to talk Grace into quitting her job at the hospital, but she wouldn't agree to it. We might need, she said, all the money we could lay our hands on soon. It was a bad place to work, but for me, not for her; she hadn't been affected by it like I had. As for the business about Mr. Peckham being my father, that was part of a well-organized delusion; she'd be my partner otherwise, but not in a *folie-a-deux*. She'd call as soon as she got home and quit if I would do the same, but otherwise the answer was no.

When I persisted she said the best she could do was to give them two weeks' notice, otherwise she would have trouble getting another job. It wouldn't look good when she got her reference. Hospitals were very particular about that sort of thing. At the end of the week she would give them two weeks' notice.

She didn't mention it, but that meant she would be working until after the conference.

I gave up. If Mr. Peckham had taken a fancy to her, quitting her job wouldn't help. That she was now his daughter-in-law wouldn't make much difference either, for he had a disregard for convention and rules that transcended immorality.

We stopped at a little restaurant off the highway and Grace surprised me by saying,

"If you want to wear your glasses I'll lead you in."

Her voice gave her away. She talked that way to patients; it was what had caused me to notice her the first day on the ward. I guessed she was trying to make me comfortable and get me home where she could get help quickly if I got worse.

"No," I took them off, "I need them most when I'm riding in the car. The scenes change so fast there must be thousands of things I've saved myself from having to remember."

"Of course," she said.

The next morning I stopped at the nurses' station and asked if there had been any calls for me while I was away.

"The typical doctor," Mrs. Bailey said. "The honeymoon is forgotten and he's all business again."

Dr. Shields slapped me on the shoulder. "Congratulations. Did you know your pay goes up two hundred dollars?"

"When are you getting a raise?" Mrs. Bailey asked him.

"I'm not going to get married until I've been in practice and have some wealthy debutantes in psychoanalysis," he said.

"When the right girl comes along you'll forget all that," Mrs. Bailey said.

"That's so," he said. "It won't make any difference how much money there is in the family—as long as they're millionaires."

Mrs. Bailey laughed. So did I, though what he'd said hadn't been altogether a joke.

The practical and efficient Mrs. Bailey revealed a surprising sentimental streak when she learned that Grace was giving notice at the end of the week.

"It's the right choice," she told me. "She will need all her energy and time for the role of little homemaker. But she'll find she will want to come back to nursing when the birds leave the nest."

What was she talking about I wondered and gently entered her mind.

In the dusty grass beside an unpaved street four young people, twin boys and twin girls, laughed and talked together.

Behind them was a gate in a white picket fence. A cement walk with grass growing from the cracks went back under the interlacing boughs of two big old cherry trees to where, one step up, was the porch of a small white frame house. The girls wore blue-checked cotton dresses of midi-length, and the boys, sweatshirts and corduroy pants. Each carried a tattered alligator Gladstone bag. They were waiting for the bus to college and Life. The girls, except that their hair hung in coiled ringlets down over their shoulders, were replicas of Grace; the boys had crew cuts but otherwise resembled Dr. Shields.

I rarely turned to that sort of prying. Too often I was made uncomfortable, and then too it was an unnecessary burden on what I still feared might be my limited capacity for awareness. If I were to enter many minds like I'd just done and added their impressions to my own, I felt I'd be risking some sort of cerebral explosion.

The words and numbers came in the irregular schedule they had followed from the beginning. I made no attempt to act on them or interpret the meanings.

Grace and I went nowhere except back and forth to work, and then I wore the glasses and kept cotton stuffed in my ears.

One evening she asked if I shouldn't be preparing for the conference.

"How would I prepare?"

"Shouldn't you be making notes or something?"

"Why should I have notes when I know everything that's happened and when, too, right to the second?" It was true; the recollections included a precise knowledge of distance and time.

She looked at me, trying to comprehend. "Tell me what it's like again."

There were lines on her face that hadn't been there a few weeks before, lines etched by the tension of what to her, with her days at the hospital and her nights in the apartment, must have seemed an unending exposure to madness.

Seized by an ineffable feeling of love and tenderness, I took her hand with its long, almost untapered fingers and lacquered nails.

"It's been a bad time for you," I said. "You didn't deserve to be caught in all this."

"It will be nice when you're well again," she said. "That's certain."

Strange, I thought, when I was what she called "well" she hadn't seen me though I'd been about, and now she was almost as much a part of the "illness" as Mr. Peckham. I wouldn't care to be "well" like I'd been before it had started.

I explained again how my consciousness was extending longitudinally farther and farther into my childhood, and like a flooding stream was spreading too, so that more and more detail was being included.

"And can you still read minds?" she asked.

"Yes."

"Can you read mine now?"

"I don't want to," I said. "Too often it's unpleasant, and I don't mean yours. I have decided that telepathy at the present stage of man's evolution would not be a viable mutation."

"What do you mean?"

"Simply that in my experience in these few days, it's been so unpleasant and demoralizing that if a child were born with it and didn't have extraordinary capabilities otherwise, like for instance Mr. Peckham, it wouldn't survive. Perhaps the last great mutation of our species resulted in the speech center of the brain, but with speech used as often to conceal as to reveal, a telepath would find the discrepancies between thought and speech intolerable, and he'd go mad. I used to think that might have happened to Mr. Peckham, but I don't believe it now."

"Tell me what you do believe about him."

"You don't really want to hear," I said, and got a startled look, but it had only been a guess.

47

WHEN, AT LAST, I was sitting in the front row of the auditorium and Dr. Hahn had started his drawn-out introduction, I felt surprise that we had been allowed to proceed so far. A crowd was gathered to hear about Mr. Peckham, and his sister had once said, "Ernest does not like attention."

It was a warm afternoon (in the article about this conference Dr. Palmer is preparing he contends that because the weather kept the less compulsive away, a biased sample of the staff was present) and attendance was less than usual. Of the 202 seats in the room, 147 were empty.

There was a shuffling of feet and shifting of bodies in chairs when Dr. Hahn stepped down and I took his place. I intentionally began with familiar staff conference phrases.

"The case to be presented today is that of E.P., a fifty-five-year-old asthenic white male who is unresponsive to all stimuli and seems totally withdrawn. I will not give the history as it appears on the chart. It is typical of schizophrenia beginning in childhood and following a relentless downhill course to complete deterioration. A careful physical examination showed no abnormalities, but by chance I did discover some peculiar findings. I have a strip of film that demonstrates these, but first we will see some slides."

I asked that the lights be dimmed. They would see objective evidence now. It would be surprising, but it would be the sort of stuff they usually dealt with. It would be something to hold to when I led them into a fantastic and unfamiliar world.

"The first slide shows the results of laboratory work done on E.P. in this hospital. Notice the dates. There are no entries between his admission and readmission and then none until recently. There was no reason to order more. He has never had a complication, an infection, or even an elevation of temperature in the twenty-five years he has been here. Notice also how nearly identical these findings are. Either his metabolism has not varied at all or our lab reports the same results on all specimens.

"To eliminate the last possibility, I sent some specimens to a private lab and others I examined myself.

"The next slide, please.

"You see that the results are the same. On the last line are the weights of stools he passed; these all weighed 184 grams.

"The next slide will be the last we will see for a while. This was also prepared in a private laboratory and is a diagram of E.P.'s chromosome count. The circled pair are extra, for E.P. has two more than the usual compliment of forty-six chromosomes. Those duplicated are the No. 2 pair, which give to this abnormality the title 'Tetrasomy two.' This has never been reported before, and were it the only unusual finding in this patient would make him worthy of being presented here as well as the subject of an article for the literature."

Had I stopped as I was tempted to and answered a few questions, it would have been a short but successful conference, and I would never know if I'd acted voluntarily.

"As you are aware," I continued, "patients who have supernumerary chromosomes almost invariably have profound alterations in the structure or function of the central nervous system. Examples are the mental retardation in Down's syndrome and the psychopathic behavior reported in Klinefelter's syndrome. In the case of E.P., since the second pair of chromosomes are much larger than those involved in either of these conditions, we can logically expect an even greater deviation from normal, and yet all we are told in the brief history is that he was precocious.

"E.P. was precocious, all right; we might as well call him that as anything else, for no words in the English language can describe nor human mind grasp what his real powers are. What's on the chart is a public relations story, not a history. You'll hear the real history though, if he'll let me finish; it's hard to believe I could get this far. I've pieced it together from the recollections of E.P.'s sister (paradoxically, her own psychosis serves to validate what she tells us) and from a weird train of circumstances and from some pretty wild experiences of my own."

This wasn't the way I'd planned the presentation and I stopped altogether for eighteen seconds. Except for a few laughs that had surprised me when I'd said the lab might make the same report on all specimens, the audience had been quiet and attentive. Now they were absolutely still.

Taking care to avoid any particular face, I directed my thoughts to them.

Prepare for a shock. What you will hear will be mind stretching. Remember the true scientist can abandon established ideas.

"Imagine," I began again, "a person possessing a colossal intelligence many orders of magnitude greater than what we call genius. Imagine also that the experience of mankind—as the puzzles of nature and the universe have been unraveled, others more complex and fascinating have been revealed—is also true for this person, but on a scale infinitely grander, so that available to him is an endlessly intricate and absorbing pastime that is incomprehensible to those about him.

"What sort of life would he choose? He would avoid recognition, for that would mean notoriety and would surely interfere with his meditation. He would talk to no one, for no one could understand what he would bother to say. He would live in a way that allowed him the most possible freedom from the chores that occupy the rest of us day by day.

"Just as many of our geniuses are considered eccentric in their preoccupation, he would be considered hopelessly insane, and he would welcome that. He'd leave his body in expert hands at some hospital and travel light to a private frontier of perpetually developing beauty.

"You may ask, what is so different about E.P.'s psychosis from any other schizophrenic? Perhaps it is only that he has no delusions: His power is real.

"If we could have the lights dimmed again, I have one more slide.

"That I knew nothing of this article until a week ago and then discovered it—like Mercury's perturbations were discovered—because I guessed that the event it describes might have happened, should impress you. Surely circumstantial evidence gains respectability when it is predicted.

"The first paragraph concerns us most.

'Eminent Physician Dies
The verse of Job "The Lord giveth and the Lord hath taken away" was never more aptly illustrated than it was last night at the untimely demise of Dr. Frederick Danishek. He had barely delivered a fine, healthy son to Mrs. W. B. Peckham when he, himself, was stricken with an apoplectic seizure and died almost at once.'

"The rest is of no interest to us except for this line, 'Dr. Danishek, age fifty-two, had seemed in the robust vigor of the prime of life.'"

Uneasiness had come to the dim room. Here and there heads were bent in whispered consultation, and people in the front turned now and then and looked back up at the others behind them. I raised my voice and went on.

"We have the word of E.P.'s sister that he knew something of the world he was to arrive in, but she could not warn him how he would be greeted. And the eminent physician could not know, the hearty slap on the buttocks that ordinarily brought an angry cry and was supposed to make the baby breathe would this time bring a devastating jolt of pure anger that would take his own breath forever."

"Dr. Boyd, could I interrupt a moment, Dr. Boyd?" Dr. Hahn was standing in the front row.

"Since I'm liable to run over the time a little," I said, "I think it best if we save all questions until the end. Could I have the movie projector turned on, please?"

Dr. Hahn sat down as the title lit up the screen "Regular EBI (eye-blink interval), a Pathognomonic Sign of the Tetrasomy Two Syndrome."

I'd had a professional photographer film a closeup of Mr. Peckham's face with my hand beside it working a stopwatch. To get in more EBI's the action was speeded up, which made it harder to tell the sequence of events and made the eyelid movements look unnaturally fast. One got the impression that the watch and eyes were geared together and that the second-hand swinging down snapped the lids shut and open again.

While the film ran, I explained why blinking was necessary and how I'd happened to discover that E.P.'s EBI was regular.

"For the rest of us," I said, "the involuntary functions—the pulse, the blood pressure, eye-blinking, breathing, even our digestion—are affected by what happens around us, but for him, who never had emergencies to meet or even any concerns, these are useless and primitive mechanisms that may not even be part of his physiology. I rather think, though, that what we are seeing is total somatic control and that he set these functions to operate precisely when he absented himself, as we set the thermostat in our house when we go on vacation."

Perforations appeared in the mechanized face, the screen glowed white, and the film clacked in the projector.

With the lights on again, I told the complete story of Mr. Peckham. I began with the questions his sister had been asked before he was born and then gave her description of life in the Peckham household. I told them how his parents had sacrificed themselves in an effort to destroy him. I explained that some people—Samuel Holden, the orderly at Harbor Hospital, and Mr. Vukov—had been aware of his commands, but others—my mother and Mrs. Bailey, when she had canceled the ambulance—had not. I listed the messages I had received and described their effect on me, and finally I told them of what had happened to my mother when she had worked at the sanitarium.

"I debated," I said, ten minutes past the usual time for ending, "whether or not to tell you of this only partly because I feared you would not believe me. My greater concern was what I was doing to you. Knowledge of E.P. has been dangerous and, if it still is, now you share that danger. But aside from that, it's a shattering experience to know such a being exists. My reason for subjecting you to this is that for some time I have been concerned that my actions were not voluntary. This formal presentation of my observations made in the tradition of our science and according to the precepts of my training is my declaration of autonomy. To you who must suffer the consequences, I can only say, 'In much wisdom is much grief and he that increaseth knowledge increaseth sorrow.' "

48

IT WAS A SOLEMN ENDING that fitted the occasion, but now that I'd reached it my audience, who had been quiet since they had settled back to watch the film, sat silently regarding me as though they expected me to go on. I resisted an impulse to sample the thoughts in front of me, for I'd played the hare once to far fewer minds.

"Are there any questions?" I asked, and when no hands were raised I did as I've seen other lecturers do, I began asking questions myself.

"Does Tetrasomy two confer a psycopathy similar to that of Klinefelter's syndrome? At first glance, the answer is an unequivocal yes, for E.P. burned his parents and systematically crippled his sister. Certainly the burden of proof would be on those who would deny it."

I paused; still no hands went up. "Why is he allowing this

discussion?" I asked. "I confess I don't know, but in spite of my brave words of a few minutes ago, I suspect that what he allows is—as no doubt was the case in the death of his parents—what he wants."

I finally turned to Dr. Hahn. "I believe you had a question, Doctor."

"Did I?" He looked around him. "Yes, I was going to stop you; now I wish I had. We can't have this sort of thing. You're endangering the hospital. He'll have to be gotten out of here. I've always said, 'The welfare of the hospital comes first.'"

"I don't think he'll permit that, sir," I said.

Now there were several questions:

"Shouldn't we notify the federal government so that troops can be stationed about the hospital, for what if the Russians acquired E.P.?"

I explained that even if we learned to communicate with him it was doubtful if he would concern himself with international problems.

Three other hands dropped after my answer.

Had I meant, I was asked now, that there was any doubt about his being a psychopath?

"I am not sure that any of our usual terms apply," I answered. "A psychopath has no loyalty to his peers, but E.P. has no peers, or none that we know of, at least."

Did I think then that there were others like him?

"There could be," I answered, "I expect that when E.P.'s case history is published, there will be a flurry of chromosome counting on patients who have been diagnosed as chronic deteriorated schizophrenics."

There was a pause then before the next hand went up. Had I had a blood type done on myself and E.P.?

"No, I have not," I said. "However, I have had a chromosome count done on myself, and the abnormality does exist in me as a mosaic. Half of my cells have double the No. 2 chromosomes." There was silence. No hands were raised.

I continued, "When a chromosome abnormality exists as a mosaic the subject is more often normal than not."

There were still no questions, and I was glad then that I'd learned to keep out of minds.

"Which brings us," I said, "to what we will call the second part of the demonstration. I once tried to establish telepathic contact with E.P. and was unsure of the result, but that was before I had the ability that I have now. You have asked me many questions about E.P. that I couldn't answer and these are only what you have thought of off-hand, as it were. There must be much that we can learn from him.

"I propose now," I said, "to try to establish contact again. Needless to say, I hope I can bring you good news."

One hour and thirty-eight minutes later the first person got up and left the room.

49

I WAS STILL in the room and everywhere else. By everywhere I mean all of the earth and our Solar System and out into the vast quiet between the stars and to the nearest stars and beyond. So, three hours and thirty-nine minutes later (there were less than half the people still waiting in the room), when they carried me on a stretcher to where I am now, two doors away from Mr. Peckham, I didn't leave the auditorium any more than I came here.

I learned about Mr. Peckham, more than I can describe, and of what I've been able to describe, more than most people will believe. Still, nine residents have resigned, which is why they are letting me out of here; my psychopathology is contagious.

I used to wonder if Mr. Peckham was lonely, and he was once, but not since he was six. Then in dreams the first faint voices spoke to him of other creatures who had dwelled on other worlds. That in physical details they had been dissimilar to him and to each other didn't matter. They had been alike: Each possessed an unimaginably immense intelligence.

The words in the messages were the constellations of origin of these beings, and each number a year when a signal reached earth that one had attained a special kind of maturity. By converting everything about them into energy in a process that we have often observed and called a nova, they had preceded Mr. Peckham into a state of pure—we have no better word—mind. They will take part in the occasion when Mr. Peckham will consume his body and our Solar System and, as a larva finally becomes a butterfly, be altogether free to take his place among them.

What no one can quite believe is that I could have gone too, and I didn't want that. If this has proved anything it's proved what I said about the individual with a mosaic pattern of chromosomes being nearer normal than otherwise. I chose a few weeks with Grace rather than eternity without her. And so when they put the electrodes on my head (the accepted treatment for what they thought was catatonic stupor) and called me back from the interstices of time and space, I came willingly.

Why did Mr. Peckham allow me to return? If a child sulks and doesn't want to attend a graduation and wedding combined, he's left at home. There is too much excitement in the preparations out there to worry about me.

Grace and I will find another beach where there aren't so many polyethylene bags and wait together, she for me to get well and I for the night to light up. That's when it's coming, at night. On that night after eighteen minutes there will be no life on Earth, and two and a half days later, no Earth.

In three years Mr. Peckham will go with the others to Cassiopeia.